May You Have Delicious Meals

May You Have Delicious Meals

JUNKO TAKASE

Translated from the Japanese by

MORGAN GILES

HUTCHINSON
HEINEMANN

HUTCHINSON HEINEMANN

UK | USA | Canada | Ireland | Australia
India | New Zealand | South Africa

Hutchinson Heinemann is part of the Penguin Random House group of companies whose addresses can be found at global.penguinrandomhouse.com

Penguin Random House UK,
One Embassy Gardens, 8 Viaduct Gardens, London SW11 7BW

penguin.co.uk
global.penguinrandomhouse.com

Penguin Random House UK

First published in Japan by Kodansha Ltd in 2022
This English translation first published in the UK by Hutchinson Heinemann in 2025
001

Typeset in 13.5/16pt Garamond MT Std by Jouve (UK), Milton Keynes
Printed and bound in Great Britain by Clays Ltd, Elcograf S.p.A.

The authorised representative in the EEA is Penguin Random House Ireland, Morrison Chambers, 32 Nassau Street, Dublin D02 YH68

A CIP catalogue record for this book is available from the British Library.

ISBN: 978–1–529–15389–7

www.greenpenguin.co.uk

MIX
Paper | Supporting responsible forestry
FSC® C018179
FSC www.fsc.org

Penguin Random House is committed to a sustainable future for our business, our readers and our planet. This book is made from Forest Stewardship Council® certified paper.

May You Have Delicious Meals

Ten minutes before lunchtime, the boss said, 'I feel like noodles today. C'mon, I'll get the car – you guys come too.' He took a few people with him and headed off to a soba place near the motorway, leaving Nitani and Fuji alone in the office.

'I'm gonna eat,' said Fuji, taking out his bento. Nitani poured some water from the kettle into a pot noodle, his standard lunch. He opened the fridge and saw two ready-made bentos from the convenience store in there. The boss must know that some people bring their own lunch, but still he said, c'mon, everyone, let's go, like it was nothing. Nitani took out a carton of green tea and shut the refrigerator door.

'C'mon, everyone, let's go, hey, what do you mean you're not coming? That's a bit antisocial,' the boss had grumbled, then suddenly added with forced joviality, 'Boss's orders!' It hardly took a genius to see that some people who didn't actually want to go would reluctantly go along with it, so the fact that the boss just ignored that was amazing, Nitani thought, genuinely impressed. 'Everything tastes better when everyone's together' – that was the boss's catchphrase. Nitani remembered running into Ashikawa coming out of the bathroom looking pale after she'd been out to eat katsudon with the boss one time. 'I tried to keep up with his pace but eating that fast makes my stomach hurt,' she'd said, one hand pressed to her stomach, still clutching a handkerchief. No doubt she'd brought her own lunch too. He'd seen her taking a bento – so small that every time he saw it he was surprised someone could need so little food – out from the lowest drawer of her desk.

Nitani opened the lid of his pot noodle. The steam was hot against his fingertips.

'Good thing we've got that meeting right after lunch, eh?' Fuji said, grinning. Nitani bowed his head vaguely at what he thought was a quick speed, which Fuji seemed to interpret as a nod, signalling agreement, conveying none of the intended vagueness. Fuji said, 'Right?' in an even stronger voice, and this time Nitani bowed more firmly.

Fuji ate his lunch, playing with his smartphone in his left hand. He had a piece of omelette in his chopsticks – not the yellow, smooth, homogenised kind Nitani often bought premade from the supermarket, but one you could tell was homemade from its colour, all white and yellow and speckled with brown. Must be nice, Nitani thought; he does as much overtime as me but when he goes home he gets food like this without even asking, all his breakfasts and lunches made for him, he can just live without even having to think about eating. Though Nitani was jealous that Fuji didn't have to think about preparing food, everything else that came along with it seemed like a real pain in the arse. Pot noodles aren't so bad, all things considered. They fill you up, anyway. But they say they're bad for you if you eat nothing else, so there's that. I wish I could eat pot noodles three meals a day and still meet all the dietary requirements for a healthy life. Or that there was a pill you could take once a day that had all the nutrients and calories you needed. You wouldn't need anything else, though food would still exist, just as a luxury product. Like cigarettes and alcohol, it'd be available to anyone who really wanted it – as Nitani ran through the thoughts he'd had so many times before, his eyes settled softly on Fuji and his surroundings.

Fuji tossed three slices of omelette in his mouth one after the other and stood up, still chewing. Nitani guessed from the way his eyes motioned towards the refrigerator that he wanted some tea. Fuji left his desk and headed towards the refrigerator, then quickly stopped. In front of Ashikawa's desk. Without a moment's hesitation, he reached out for the half-finished bottle of tea on her desktop, twisted off the lid, and drank. Noticing Nitani watching him, Fuji smiled impishly like a child caught being naughty and said, 'Man, I was so thirsty.' Nitani nodded slowly.

Fuji returned the bottle to Ashikawa's desk. It looked like it had hardly been touched. If he really had drunk from it because he was so incredibly thirsty, then he would've taken two or three sips, but he'd drunk so little that he'd just moistened his lips. Ashikawa is a young woman, Nitani thought, turning obvious facts over in his head. Fuji is a middle-aged man. I've never asked him his age, but he's the assistant branch chief so he must be over forty. Maybe it's not about age. Who knows. Is it a gender thing? Sure seems like it. Right?

Fuji took a new bottle of green tea out of the refrigerator, went back to his desk and drank from it as he started to talk about the client who would be coming in that afternoon. It was a consultation for a new label for an existing product that hadn't changed its branding in a long time. Nitani slurped his noodles as he used his left hand to operate the mouse and bring up the brief on his monitor, giving it a final once-over. As he went to pour out the remains of the soup from his pot noodle in the sink, he casually looked at Ashikawa's desk. The bottle of tea that Fuji had drunk from was sitting on top of a flower-patterned coaster.

A little after lunch was supposed to end, the rest of the team returned. Shortly before the door opened, Nitani could hear the commotion of people talking coming straight up the corridor. 'We're ba-ack,' trilled Harada, one of the part-time staff, as she walked through the door, then turned to Fuji and Nitani and announced, 'The soba was so good, and he paid for it too, for everyone!'

Behind her walked in Ashikawa, who added, 'It's so true what he always says – everything really does taste better when everyone's together.'

'That's generous of you,' Nitani said, looking at the boss's face as Fuji redid his necktie in preparation for the afternoon's clients.

'It's nothing,' the boss nodded, looking proud. 'They'll be here soon,' he added, indicating that everyone should get back to work. Nitani nodded and started to head towards the reception area on the opposite side of the partition, but Fuji stopped, so he stopped too.

'Oh, Ashikawa?' Fuji said. 'Uh, the bottle of tea there on your desk, it's a new brand that just went on sale recently, right? I was curious so – sorry – I took a little sip of it.'

Immediately Harada said reproachfully, 'Not again, Fuji, that's so gross,' but she was ignored. Nitani saw Oshio at the desk next to Ashikawa's, her face contorted in disgust.

'Oh, right,' Ashikawa said, drawing the words out, then picked up the bottle. 'What'd you think?' she asked Fuji.

He tilted his head, smiling, and said, 'It's a bit like Sokenbicha, but maybe a little more bitter.'

She took off the cap and took a sip. 'I see what you mean.'

'Oh my God, just throw it away already,' Harada said, then laughed, 'Fuji, you're awful.' Ashikawa chuckled, while Nitani stayed silent with a half-smirk on his face; he thought about how surely Ashikawa already knew how the tea tasted, so she hadn't needed to try it again, and how everyone would've been happier if she'd just said, 'It is a little bitter, isn't it?' Her drinking from it again in front of Fuji was her way of saying that what he'd done hadn't bothered her. As expected, Fuji grinned and headed out to reception, while Harada looked exasperated but said nothing else. Oshio had already lost interest and turned to her computer. Ashikawa looked Nitani in the eyes.

'Hope your meeting goes well,' she said, holding up her fists in front of her chest and shaking them.

When I told him I hated Ashikawa, Nitani smiled. I know he did too. I mean I think he did, but his expression changed in an instant so I'm starting to doubt myself. And I don't mean about whether he smiled or not, but about whether he likes me more than her.

On our way back from an off-site training course, just

when we were about to reach the station, Nitani had said, 'Well, I'm gonna get some dinner so I'll see you tomorrow.' It was just after five, and the area around the station was filled not with office workers but young people, university students and schoolkids in uniform. We were about half an hour away from the office by the train towards Tokyo, so it wasn't exactly the big city, but it was more bustling than where our office was, in the arse-end of Saitama.

'I've never been here before but you seem to know your way around,' I said, and he shook his head.

'I was just going to pick a bar at random so it might not be the kind of place ladies like, but if you don't have any other plans, wanna join me?'

His phrasing was the perfect casual invitation to a co-worker, so I said yes. Nitani walked around the cluster of bars and restaurants near the station for a little while, then said, 'This'll do,' and went in a chain restaurant on the second floor of a mixed-use building.

We'd gulped down a pint each and were on the verge of finishing our second when we'd more or less concluded shit-talking the boss. Nitani ran through all of the stories of what a self-centred, arrogant, old-fashioned bastard the boss was, the rumours about the part-timer he'd apparently had an affair with who didn't work there anymore, lots of his complaints about work; then, as if to put a cap on it, he added, 'Well, everyone knows all of that anyway.' I wondered if Nitani was more dissatisfied with Fuji, the boss's assistant who gave Nitani most of his orders, so I gently tried to ask him, but he said, 'Oh, you know,' and went no further. I couldn't tell if he'd decided there was a line beyond which he wouldn't go with a subordinate, or if he simply hadn't opened up to me yet.

Our laughter reached a peak then gradually died down, and as we sighed we reached for our beer glasses. Nitani drank first and I lifted my glass as if following his lead. The coaster underneath, branded with the restaurant's logo, was soaking wet. I brought the glass up to my face, and just before I touched my lips to it, I said, 'You know who I can't stand? Ashikawa.' He stopped drinking and looked at me. His eyes smiled for a second as if he'd let down his guard.

I took a sip, my eyes still on his. If I drank slowly it might sound worse, so I purposefully drank a little quicker, gulp gulp gulp, and downed the rest in one. As if I'd said something I hadn't meant to. 'Huh,' Nitani said, and narrowed his eyes. So we're getting it all out today, his eyes said. The pursing of his lips might have been in preparation for ridiculing.

'I need more beer,' he said, tapping on the tablet to order another drink and some fried fish bites. 'You want another?' He held the tablet out to me. I tapped the button for a whisky highball on the photo menu, and the waiter brought it over right away. The AC was too strong and I was getting a little cold. I took my jacket out of my bag and put it over my shoulders.

'What is it you can't stand about her?' He asked not why but what, which put me at a little more ease.

'Lots of things, really, but for example, the way she didn't come on the course today.'

'Oh. Mm.'

Nitani nodded once as if he understood, but after a pause he exhaled, as if he was thinking about something.

Ashikawa was supposed to have gone to the same off-site training that Nitani and I had gone to that day. We were meant to learn about laws and regulations related to work, and a ton of study materials were provided in advance, which Fuji had advised us needed to be read if we were to have any chance of keeping up, so I read them little by little over a couple of weeks. I'd just checked with Ashikawa a few days before to make sure she'd read everything. Yesterday, I'd received an email reminder from the organiser, which said, 'Since so many people are attending tomorrow, to make the most of this opportunity, I'd like to make the second half of the day dedicated to group work, which will also serve as an opportunity to network with people from other companies,' so it would've been embarrassing to show up with a low level of understanding of the material. We rarely did courses with people from other companies too. So I was a little worried anyway. That morning, when I was on the train heading to the venue, I got a message from Ashikawa. It said she wasn't feeling well so she wouldn't be there.

'She pulled out of the course we did in February on the day of too, right? The day before I didn't get the feeling like she was dreading it, but then all of a sudden . . .'

'That does seem to happen sometimes. She gets overwhelmed and calls in sick. I mean, I'm just guessing, but she's probably not great with large groups in the first place. So like this time, when she was told the day before that there's going to be groupwork involved. I guess sudden changes in plans must be hard for her to adjust to.' He took a sip of his beer and continued. 'When you said you couldn't stand her, I thought maybe she'd said or done something to you. But you just don't like her because she's not competent?'

'More like, because everyone knows she isn't, I guess,' I said, taking a drink too. Washing out my throat with alcohol. 'What you said before, about her not being good with sudden changes in plan, I think you just might be right, but then she's never said that herself, has she? She never outright says, "I can't do this because I'm not good with this kind of thing." But the boss, and Fuji, and everyone else, and you too, even though you've only been at our branch for three months, you all know it. And you make allowances for her. That's the thing that just really pisses me off.'

'Mm, but, you know, that's just the way things are nowadays.'

'I do know. But it pisses me off.'

'I get it, I'm judgemental,' I muttered to myself, but Nitani didn't let it slide.

'I don't think you are,' he said, his expression unchanged. 'She's on the same salary as you, but people make allowances for her and not for you, by which I mean, it feels like you have to make up for her, and that annoys you. I get it.'

Nitani drained his third pint as he spoke, then tapped on the tablet to order again. Another beer. He drank a lot more than he ate.

'Some people aren't up to it, but then if nobody does the work, then the company can't function. So the people who are capable do it, and they do it all. Then those people might get promoted, but just because they can actually do their job doesn't mean they want a promotion, right? They're just doing what needs to be done. Two of the guys who got hired at the same time as me, they've already had to take a leave of absence. And then when they do come back to work, they'll probably be reassigned to general admin.' The department with the least amount of overtime, to which people with physical or mental issues were most likely to be transferred. 'They can go home when they're supposed to every day, but they get the same bonus we do. They'll never get promoted, but if they just kind of hang in there until retirement, they're all set. What more could you want?'

'What more could you want?' I muttered. This time Nitani didn't pick up on what I mumbled to myself. His voice was getting a little louder. Maybe he was starting to get drunk. The waiter brought over some edamame.

'Didn't we have edamame already? Did you get another one?'

'I realised I need to eat some vegetables.'

Then order a salad, I thought, but I got it – when you're drinking beer you don't want lettuce, you want something salty to snack on. I picked up an edamame pod too. Nitani pushed the empty plate he was using for the shells closer to me. The edamame seemed to have been refrigerated after cooking, so it was cold and tender all the way through.

'The guys you're talking about, they irritate me too, but maybe I'm also, like, a little jealous. Well, not quite. 'Cause I definitely don't want to end up like them. But I wouldn't say I hate them either.'

'But you said you can't stand Ashikawa, right?'

'Maybe if we didn't work together I wouldn't hate her.

I mean, she seems nice enough, right? Though I don't have any friends like her in real life, so if it weren't for work I'd probably have nothing to do with her.'

'Then if you weren't co-workers you probably would've never met.'

'Yeah. Maybe I was destined to hate her.'

'Destined,' Nitani sputtered. He had some edamame in his mouth, which he hurried to put a hand over. I burst out laughing at the sight. God, you're drunk, I thought. Doesn't take much to make you laugh now. The phrase 'laugh at the roll of a chopstick' came to mind, and I gently rolled one of my chopsticks on the table. He saw and laughed again. 'What're you doing? Ridiculous,' he chuckled. This was fun. Making him produce more and more laughter. It was a real belly laugh. He snorted.

'Too much fun,' I said, and Nitani put his hand to his forehead and let out a deep breath. It put me at ease seeing him like this. I'd never seen him laugh like this at any work drinks. Suddenly I leaned in to the table, bringing my face closer to his.

'So what do you say, do you want to bully Ashikawa with me?'

Nitani bent his head to the right, as if he was stretching his neck muscles, pushing his left ear towards the ceiling. He smiled with cold eyes, leaning at an unfamiliar angle. No, maybe his eyes aren't cold after all. He's just drunk and trying to keep it together, which is what's making him stare like that. Because why would he be looking at me like that otherwise? And so on and on my thoughts went, but just as I finally panicked and opened my mouth to say, 'Just kidding,' Nitani said, 'Sure.' See, it was fine. All good. I lifted my highball, which was nearly empty.

'Cheers!' I said, tapping it against the pint glass Nitani was holding.

'Glass's empty again.' Nitani twisted his mouth in dissatisfaction.

I smiled and reached for the tablet. 'Well, let's have another. And then maybe another after that. I'm having a great time,' I said, hitting Nitani's arm to rub it.

Nitani imagined that Oshio had bested Ashikawa pretty soon after starting at their company. Their company mainly produced labels and packaging for food and beverage products, and in addition to the head office in Tokyo where the design department was located, it also had eight branches nationwide with sales departments including the one where Nitani and his team worked. Oshio had been hired right out of university five years ago; Ashikawa had been there six years now. Oshio had been teamed up with Ashikawa straightaway. Even their desks were right next to each other. She must've liked Ashikawa at the start, he guessed. She'd have been relieved to have someone so nice there to mentor her. But by the time she'd been there six months, she'd probably gotten fed up.

That's how it'd been for Nitani. He'd been hired there a year before Ashikawa joined and had spent six years at a branch in the north-east. Three months ago he'd been transferred to the Saitama branch, and he was supposed to learn the ropes from Ashikawa. But about two weeks after his transfer he'd already had the thought: I'm gonna overtake her in no time at all, easy. It's hard to respect someone after that. Without that smidgen of respect, you can't sustain the simple affection you need to have for your colleagues, who, after all, are not people you choose to spend your time with because you like them.

In April when Nitani was transferred, he made a mistake on a job he'd just taken over from Ashikawa. He hadn't been informed that a delivery was supposed to be made a day early, and when the client called asking when it would arrive, he'd rushed there to apologise, then got the items delivered the next day. Luckily the delivery coming a day late hadn't seemed to matter, and he'd got off lightly by giving the client a large box of sweets. The wrong delivery date had been listed on the documents that Nitani had received. When he double-checked later, the date written in the email that Ashikawa had sent to him was the correct one. She'd apologised to him over and over again, but Nitani thought it was his own fault for not being thorough enough, so he told her so. What had bothered him was that she hadn't accompanied him to apologise in person, and Fuji had been the one to call. 'Mr Nitani, the staff member currently assigned to your account, will be coming to see you,' he'd said, which was how Nitani had learned he was going. He'd thought that perhaps that was why Fuji, who was his manager, had called, but later, Fuji explained to him, 'Apparently at the last place Ashikawa worked, she experienced some . . . harassment or something like that, and she still can't really handle men yelling at her,' which was when he learned that Ashikawa was a year older than him and was turning thirty this year.

The client was a middle-aged man with a big body and a voice to match. When Nitani handed over the box of sweets, he'd certainly been loud as he said, 'And don't let it happen again!' But he hadn't been high-handed about it.

Nitani gave up respecting Ashikawa the moment the thought that she lacked a backbone came to the surface of his mind, as murky as dirty water in the bottom of a pot left unwashed. And once he had, he felt fine imagining her as he masturbated. The strange thing was, the version of her in his mind was sexier now he could only see her faults than it had been back when he'd thought she was kind of cute. She was always crying in a kind of voice he'd never heard before. The more she cried the better.

At the Friday work drinks the day after Nitani's move to the Saitama branch, Harada, a part-timer whose name he hadn't yet committed to memory, came up to him and talked about Ashikawa and nothing but. Ashikawa was from a few stops down the train line from the office and she lived there with her family, but she was still a really good cook despite living at home, and she was good at baking too, always kind to everyone, always smiling, not a bad bone in her body, said Harada.

Nitani made a few perfunctory noises in response, thinking that Harada was probably just trying to tell him a little more about someone at work near his own age. But then if that were the case, Harada would've mentioned Oshio too, and her name hadn't come up, he thought suspiciously. Then Harada narrowed her eyes beneath her thickly pencilled-in eyebrows and asked, 'By the way, are you dating anyone?'

Nitani vaguely pictured the face of his grandmother, who was turning ninety this year. She had this and that wrong with her but her mind was still there, and whenever Nitani went to visit her at her care home, she always told him, 'I want to meet my great-grandchildren.' His little sister had a boyfriend she'd been with for a long time, so he'd tell her, 'You'll have less of a wait from her,' but she wouldn't be swayed: 'No. I want to see my bloodline continue.'

She was a traditional old lady so, to her, the continuance of the family came down to Nitani, the oldest grandson, and she'd always spoiled him. Since childhood, she would give treats only to him, and at mealtimes she would take two or three pieces of meat from her own plate and put them on his. He could still see the face of his little sister as an elementary school student, still very young, looking at him with betrayal in her eyes. That's not fair, she'd said, and in her face he saw nothing cute and rosy-cheeked but rather the merciless look of utter contempt that only a child may direct at others so openly.

Will I ever get married, Nitani wondered. Not because he wanted to, but rather because he'd never decided he didn't want to. Some people decide that they'll never get married, but that's only for those who really know their own mind, so for people like me with no real goals in life, it doesn't make sense to decide that. So then I might as well get married while there are plenty of people who'd be happy to see it happen. That's how he felt.

So when Ashikawa cried, he'd reached out to her. He'd joined in when everyone else consoled her after she'd been yelled at by another client, not the one he'd made the mistake with, telling her that she had nothing to worry about because the other party was clearly at fault and were just trying to deflect the blame. Ashikawa, told to take a break until she'd calmed down, had shut herself in the office kitchen, and when nobody else was around Nitani had gone in there too.

'You OK?' he said, as he walked up to her. 'I hope you're not crying because you think you've done something wrong. You got yelled at and you got scared, that's all.' He stood next to her as if hiding her in his own shadow. Holding a handkerchief over her eyes, Ashikawa nodded and took an audible breath.

'Nitani, I can't imagine you . . . ever yelling,' she said, very quietly.

'No matter how quietly you whisper, the people around you here will always hear what you have to say.' Nitani reached out his hand and touched her shoulder. She had the thinnest, narrowest shoulders of any woman he'd ever touched, so devoid of strength there seemed to be nothing within them.

They'd gone to see a movie on their first date. The right kind of movie, one that everyone was talking about with big flashy action scenes, the kind you could talk about how funny it was afterwards. She'd bought a souvenir pamphlet at the concession stand afterwards. 'You liked it that much?' Nitani had asked, and she'd smiled and said, 'A keepsake.' They had dinner at a restaurant known for its wine and Italian-style omelettes, then gone their separate ways.

For their second date, they'd gone into Tokyo and eaten at a Brazilian steakhouse. There, in a noisy restaurant filled with the light rhythms of Brazilian music, a waiter in a samba costume had cut meat from an iron sword and arranged it on their plates. Ashikawa was delighted. 'This is so cool – I could never've come here all by myself,' she trilled.

Their third date took place at an izakaya near Nitani's apartment. It was an old place run by an elderly couple with not much in the way of choice of drinks, but it was a fine place for drinking a bottle of beer and eating some dinner. The TV was usually showing the Giants' game. Nitani had said that he ate there a few times a week, and Ashikawa said she wanted to go, so he took her there. He waited for her at the station; she appeared wearing a grey dress, and the formal look combined with her carefully curled medium-length hair made her stand out from everyone else in the bar, but it wasn't the kind of place where people cared about appearances anyway.

'What do you usually get?'

'Bottle of beer, some edamame, grilled fish, omelette . . . and some miso soup too.'

'A proper dinner.'

Ashikawa smiled as if something were funny. Nitani had smiled back at her but inside he felt a little irritated. Well, I don't live with my parents like you do, so my mummy doesn't wait on me, you know – he felt the words coiling in his stomach, words that couldn't ever reach his mouth, washed down with the last of his beer until they dissolved. Once they'd melted away Nitani no longer remembered that they had ever existed. He would meticulously forget those words and the feelings that had given rise to them in the first place.

'This omelette's really good.'

Ashikawa's eyes widened. He thought her voice sounded louder than it ought to be to talk just to him; Ashikawa was looking over his shoulder, grinning. The old man who ran the place was there, smiling at her. Why's she getting special treatment, he thought, getting irritated again. 'Good, really good,' she repeated.

'You really do know how to make everything seem delicious,' Nitani had said, in a voice cheerful enough not to sound sarcastic, tinged with an admiration that he did truly feel.

'Do I?'

The look of having been praised appeared on her face.

A smile with gaps in its happiness, where humility might be inserted, to say: oh, that's not true.

'You like eating, anyway.'

'I suppose so. I think maybe what I like is living properly. To me, eating and sleeping, the things that are essential to life, they're not something you can like or dislike.'

You can't even let yourself dislike something, seriously? He swallowed to rid himself of the bad taste her words had suddenly left in his mouth.

'Nights when I don't eat in a bar like this, I eat something from a convenience store, and that's it. Like onigiri or a pastry or something,' he said.

Her eyes had widened in surprise. 'Oh no. Maybe you could try just making some miso soup. You just boil some water and mix in some miso, the kind that already has the stock in it, and then just add some tofu or greens. If you don't want to even have to wash up a knife, you could just scoop out as much tofu as you want from the pack with a spoon or break it up by hand, even. And the greens, you can cut them up with scissors, easy-peasy. Wouldn't your body feel happier eating something hot you made yourself?'

It fucking wouldn't, Nitani had thought, with the speed of a fist swinging to punch. Then he had remembered that she'd phrased it as a question rather than a statement, and said, 'You might be right.' If I told her that staring at a pot waiting for it to boil makes me feel like I'm being reduced down little by little, she'd never understand, he thought, feeling his jaw going slack. I fucking hate chewing. And people like Ashikawa say shit like 'easy, simple, time-saving recipes' while insisting on spending proper time with food.

Whatever, we're probably going to have sex tonight, he thought. He looked at Ashikawa, who was bringing a piece of omelette topped with grated daikon up to her mouth. Nitani thought that the reason he hadn't made a move before the third date was because they worked together and if he wasn't careful there could be trouble later, but, in fact, Nitani had previously slept with women in the same office who were part-time or on fixed-term contracts, so it would be inaccurate to say that was the main reason. This was not to say that he hadn't had any problems with any of the women he'd had relationships with in the past, but for the most part, things had ended by mutual agreement, without a nasty breakup. They had worked at the same office, been single, and likely to move on to other branches in a few years, and on the face of things this was no different, but what made Nitani cautious was how Ashikawa's fragility made her untouchable. One could say that was Nitani's type. He liked unreliable, weak-seeming, sweet girls, especially ones that were delicate and slim, with no hint of a 'bite' in their expressions, but he found himself most strangely drawn to the boldness of their weakness, the declaration that they ought to be protected.

While Ashikawa was in the toilet, Nitani had settled up; he was taken aback when the old lady, who had brought him the bill, said, 'Nice of your lady friend to make a point of coming to the kitchen to say how good everything was.' Had she done this where Nitani could see, like she had with the other owner before, then he could understand and assume that the intention had been to make a good impression on their third date, but was she really like that when he wasn't looking too? Still silent, he felt at a loss. He was starting to think that this woman he was planning to make a move on was, perhaps, the type of person he couldn't see all the way through, that needed to be handled with care.

They had bought some cans of beer and bottled tea at a convenience store, then headed back to Nitani's building. Looking around his tiny studio flat, Ashikawa said admiringly, 'It's so clean,' but she also seemed aware that, knowing she would probably visit that evening, he had cleaned intensively. This gave Nitani an uncomfortable feeling he couldn't easily dismiss, but then he hated the cynical type who would say, wryly, 'Oh, I see you cleaned up for me.' So Ashikawa was right. And Nitani knew that he was making the right choice. When he'd put his arms around her, she let out a small, satisfied sigh in his embrace.

When he woke up, he had a slight headache. He never ate in the morning, but he decided to gulp down a cup of jelly he had in his fridge so he could take some painkillers. The large green grapes in it smashed in his mouth, sour. He swallowed the pills down with the dregs of the jelly, trying not to chew. By the time he left the house and started walking the drugs were starting to kick in and his headache had started to subside.

Coming out of a convenience store near the office, he ran into Ashikawa, so they walked together.

'How was the course yesterday?' Ashikawa asked.

'Fine,' was all he said. No way would he purposefully tell her he'd gone drinking with Oshio afterwards.

'That's nice,' Ashikawa said, but Nitani didn't know what exactly was supposed to be nice. That he'd done the course earnestly? She had a habit of saying 'That's nice', when she could've just said 'Right.' 'That's nice', 'must be nice', 'that's great' – all the other phrases she used were just so endearingly *her*.

'Oh, it's Fuji.'

On the other side of the street, where Ashikawa was pointing, a silver SUV waited at the lights. Fuji was in the driver's seat, looking straight ahead; he didn't seem to have noticed them. As Nitani wondered if he should wave at him, the light changed and Fuji drove on.

'He looked like he was scowling at something,' Ashikawa said. Nitani thought he'd just been making the kind of face you make when you're alone, but she continued, 'I wonder if something bad happened. Maybe he and his wife had a fight.'

'That's just how you look when you're alone, isn't it? Facial expressions are only something you do when someone else is around – that's what I think, anyway.'

'Wait, really?' Ashikawa said, surprised, putting her hand to her cheek. 'But I – I think I make faces when I'm all alone.'

Nitani nodded slightly, unsure how else to respond. Then, realising that might seem curt, he added, 'Oh yeah?'

'Smiling is supposed to be good for your health, they say. There's some chemical, I can't remember what it's called, that your body only produces when you're smiling, or something. So even when I'm alone I try to smile as hard as I can. Like a grin.'

She pulled the sides of her mouth up firmly to show him. Since he'd run into her earlier she had been smiling the whole time, though not so hard as to create dimples, like now. Nitani became conscious of his own expression. Even when he faced ahead or away from Ashikawa, the corners of his mouth naturally raised themselves. Perhaps his face was preparing itself to be acceptable to look at her. But he found it hard to believe that his body was producing any chemical beyond the ordinary.

'So just forcing a smile has that effect, huh? Like when you see something funny and laugh, that's not what does it?'

'Hm. I don't really know; I just know it's easier to keep a smile on my face.'

Nitani was about to respond when Harada called out, 'Good morning,' behind them. Letting Harada take his place next to Ashikawa, Nitani walked ahead in front of them. Occasionally he turned his head halfway to look back and join in the conversation. When he was facing ahead, he was aware that the corners of his mouth were lower than they had been before. At the same time, he realised that though he'd taken those painkillers, he still had a slight headache. Not a sharp pain, but a heavy, dull one.

Whenever he checked during work, Ashikawa did indeed always have an expression on her face. Usually she was smiling. As she looked at her computer screen or printed documents, as she washed a visitor's mug in the kitchen, her mouth was slightly upturned. Of course, if someone said her name, her mouth jerked right up, and her eyes opened wider. When she wasn't smiling her face didn't return to rest either; when she was dealing with something difficult, she had a troubled, even sad expression. She did not furrow her brows so much as lower them, and the intensity of her eyes was so diminished it was enough to unsettle anyone she looked at. She shows her emotions so clearly and yet I've never seen her get irritated once. She never glares, or sighs to get others' attention, or slams the phone down as hard as she can without it seeming violent, and when she's interrupted in the middle of doing something, she never acts as if she hadn't heard or keeps staring at her monitor as she responds lifelessly – she says, 'Sure,' cheerfully, with that same tight smile on her face.

Harada, who seemed to think she wasn't really carrying on a conversation unless she was saying what a nice person so-and-so was, often praised Ashikawa: She's smart, she's always nice to us part-timers, she loves to bake, she's cute, she's a really great girl. I wish she'd marry my son. Nitani always went along with it and agreed with her, but one day Fuji said, 'Oh, Harada, knock it off already,' while laughing. Harada had seemed hurt. 'Maybe I'm just a busybody,' she said, pouting.

Harada liked to praise Oshio too. Sometimes she said Oshio was a nice girl, like Ashikawa, but most of the time she said, 'Just what you'd expect from a former cheerleader! And from the top team in Kyushu!'

Apparently Oshio had been on the cheerleading team in high school.

Fuji had grinned. 'In one of those itsy-bitsy skirts.'

'Disgusting,' said Harada.

'It was a long time ago,' said Oshio, in a cold tone meant to end the conversation.

'But, wow, that's amazing,' said Ashikawa, softly drawing out the end of the word. The exchange careened through the whole range of sentiments and tones.

Nitani sat on the floor and leaned against the bedside table, looking at Ashikawa in the kitchen. She was cutting a carrot; only her mouth was smiling. Her gaze, directed at the ingredients, was serious; she had a more dignified look than she did even at work.

'Whatcha making?'

'White rice with corn and some mackerel.'

He didn't understand quite where the carrot came into things, but he nodded anyway. He never bought carrots except when he was making curry. He didn't know what else they could be used for. He'd never seen them in pre-mixed salads either; for that matter, he couldn't even remember the last time he'd eaten one. He ate tomatoes and lettuce occasionally, and recently they'd started selling vegetable crisps made of pumpkin so he'd eaten that. But carrot felt somehow distant. A very distant vegetable to him.

Nitani drank the carbonated water in his glass. He

wanted to watch funny videos, but he didn't feel like he could just sit there and relax while Ashikawa was cooking, so he was scrolling through news sites on his phone. Occasionally, he came across something he found interesting so he'd read it out loud to her. He lived alone so he didn't have a TV. He didn't watch much TV anyway, and if there was something he wanted to watch he could just watch it online so it didn't matter, but once he got married he should probably get a TV, he thought idly. At times like this, watching something on your phone or laptop could seem kind of anti-social, but having a TV on felt more acceptable – even if he was the one who chose the channel, it wouldn't necessarily be showing something he wanted to watch. As Nitani followed this train of thought, he realised that Ashikawa had slid naturally into his imaginings of married life, which quietly shook him, but all things considered, he would probably be best off marrying Ashikawa or someone like her anyway, he decided.

'I've never had white rice with corn in it before.'

'It's pretty good. If I'm going to mix something in rice in the summer, that's what I make.'

When they were alone together, they both sounded more relaxed, but they didn't shed all formalities. They didn't want to seem overly familiar at work, so the way they referred to each other and spoke didn't change much. It wasn't something they'd discussed and decided on together, just something that had happened naturally. So when they were intimate it was a largely wordless exchange of vowels, like oohs and aahs, and breaths. That was rather animalistic, which Nitani liked. Once the act was done, Ashikawa would go right to sleep without showering, and that was good too.

That day, after they'd eaten the white rice with corn, fried mackerel, and salad with thinly sliced quick-pickled carrot in it, they had gone to bed before the contents of their stomachs had digested, and though it was still only ten o'clock, Ashikawa had fallen asleep. He pulled the blanket over her naked body snugly up to her neck so she didn't catch cold. She slept soundly, only her head exposed. Her sleeping face, expressionless, lacked shape. It was cuter when she was awake and moving.

He got out of bed and went to the kitchen to boil some water. He didn't have a kettle so he put some water in a pot and put it on the stove. He turned the hob on low to keep the sound of the water moving in the pot as minimal as possible, so it took a long time for it to come to a boil. Occasionally he glanced over at Ashikawa to make sure she hadn't woken up. All the lights were turned off, aside from the light over the kitchen sink, which shone at an angle across Ashikawa's face. She didn't snore, so it was hard to tell whether she was actually asleep or just pretending.

He poured the boiling water into a pot noodle. Before

the three minutes were up he opened the lid, still standing in the kitchen, and the irresistible aroma rose in the form of steam towards the dark ceiling. He stuck his face in it and inhaled through his nose. The air he breathed in filled his stomach. He wanted to slurp the noodles down all at once but he didn't want to wake up Ashikawa, so he ate stealthily, playing with his phone with one hand. Once he'd eaten nearly 80 per cent of it he finally felt like he'd eaten dinner. The first time Ashikawa had come over to his place, she'd seen the stacks of pot noodles on top of his refrigerator. 'That's a lot,' she'd said, her eyes wide. He'd said that she didn't seem like the type to eat instant noodles, and she had responded, 'That's right, almost never,' with a strangely troubled look on her face. Nitani had thought: well, that's no surprise, my parents didn't let me eat this stuff when I lived with them either.

He felt satisfied now, and he hadn't really been hungry in the first place, but if he left any behind then tomorrow Ashikawa would know what he'd done, so he had no choice but to eat it all now. He took one last sip of the soup and poured the rest away. After he poured the soup out, he ran the tap for a while to wash away the smell too. He washed out the container and put it in the rubbish bag. He didn't have a bin; instead, he had a 45-litre rubbish bag sitting right on the floor. Inside were the packaging for the fish and the vegetables that Ashikawa had used, plus the end of the carrot and onion skins. She'd generated a lot more rubbish than he did buying a ready-meal at the convenience store. He shoved the container in as deep with his disposable chopsticks as he could. Somewhere deep in the strata he heard the sound of cracking plastic. Startled by the sharpness of the sound, he looked over at Ashikawa, but her eyes were still closed. Nitani listened closely, hearing as usual the soft sound of her breathing instead of any snoring, and he vaguely thought that Oshio probably snored properly.

On the way back to his from the supermarket that day, Ashikawa had yelped, 'Cat!' and pointed down the road. A grey cat was walking along the sidewalk.

'Good spot. He's pretty far away,' Nitani had said.

'I love animals,' she said, her eyes still locked on the cat. 'Whenever I'm out I just see them right away. Although I'm really a dog person.'

'Oh, right. I love dogs too. I had one when I was a kid.'

'Really? I have a dog. It's a mutt, about this big,' she said, holding up the large grocery bag in her hand to show. She was carrying the one with the lighter things in it; it was stuffed full of crisps and the pot noodles that Nitani ate when he was alone. 'He's called Mukosuke.'

'Mukosuke?'

'Yeah. He's a rescue, so we don't know his birthday, but he's ten this year. He's cute.'

'Nice,' he'd said, immediately prepared for her to ask him to come over and meet the dog sometime, but all Ashikawa said was, 'Good thing we're both dog people, huh?' The grey cat had disappeared at some point.

Satisfied that all trace of the pot noodle was gone, he slid back into bed next to Ashikawa. The sound of her breathing changed, and he wondered if she was awake, but she didn't say anything so he didn't either. He turned away from her and played with his phone, careful not to let the light from the screen reach her. She's cute, she's sweet, she can cook well, she's older than me but she seems younger; she's the kind of person who will probably act younger all her life, no matter her age. He remembered the faces of everyone he'd gone out with and fallen in love with before. She looked like all of them.

It had been about two when Ashikawa left work early. Without warning, she had got up from her desk and gone over to Fuji, who then spoke to the boss, and then she went home as if everything were perfectly normal.

When Oshio asked Fuji what to do since she and Ashikawa had been working on drafting a contract together and it might not be done in time to get approval tomorrow, Fuji said, 'It is what it is.' He seemed to be telling her that if she couldn't do it herself then too bad. The words 'Sure, but' started to come out of her mouth; she swallowed them. Instead, she apologised. Her voice sounded so pointed it surprised even her. Fuji sighed. He looked frazzled. But he'd listened to the reason for Ashikawa's early departure with a sympathetic smile on his face, Oshio thought grimly. She knew there was no point but she still felt disgusted. They would never be treated equally. The higher-ups were not teachers, carefully trained to avoid bias, so they played favourites. 'Everyone thinks they're the only one doing it right,' Fuji said. 'The people who just do the work and go home, the people who give it their all, the people who don't do overtime and the ones who do a lot of it, they all think their way is the right one.' Oshio was at a loss for words at being told she was no different.

'What can you do, right? Someone who's incapable . . . no, I don't think Ashikawa can't do the work, but, like, generally, there's a certain number of people who can't deal when things get tough, and you can't just fire them all. Well, I mean, I don't know what other companies are doing. But pretty big companies like ours just can't. It's already factored in that there's all kinds of people. So Ashikawa's fine, totally no problem. There was a guy called Maki at my old office. Mid-forties . . . maybe you've heard about him – oh, you have? Well, he was awful. "My hay fever's too bad, I'm not coming in." "My neck's too stiff, I'm not coming in." "The atmospheric pressure is low and I feel horrible so I'm going home." One thing after another. Always the kind of thing that everyone else just puts up with. And his favourite word was "rights". Workers' rights. Quality of life. "The only one looking out for you is you." I mean, I know what he was saying. By which I mean, I wish I could be like that too. But then, when one guy says he's going to take care of himself and goes home early, then who's going to do his work? Because everyone gets hay fever at the same time. So then, someone else with hay fever has to do the work of the person who went home because of their hay fever, pushing themselves, pulling overtime. And yet nobody really remarks on this, and you end up stuck between a rock and a hard place, right? Maki was married, and I think he had kids too. Two of them. His wife was a housewife. Absolutely unbelievable, right? I mean. Un-be-liev-able.'

Oshio didn't know quite what the difference between this Maki person and Ashikawa was, but what Fuji had said, about how everyone thought their way of working was right, had struck a chord. Ashikawa didn't push herself. She thought not doing what she couldn't do was right. What I think is right is different. We live by different rules.

After the official end of the workday, Oshio invited Nitani, who had gone into the break room to make a coffee, out for a drink. She suggested they leave separately at eight and meet up at a bar, to which Nitani frowned and said, 'Why? Why not go together?' After all, they were just two co-workers going for a drink after work, so why the need for secrecy? He didn't say those words, but she'd felt like he was poking his finger in her face as he spoke.

When they both stood up from their desks at the same time and said, 'See you later,' Fuji, who was peering at his monitor with his chest close to the surface of his desk, straightened up and teased them: 'What's going on here, you two going for a drink together?'

Oh shut up, Oshio thought, just as Nitani said, 'Yep. Just thought we might as well. Do you want to come too?' A noise of surprise came out of her mouth inadvertently.

'Oshio, you don't look too happy about that. Ouch. Well, then maybe I will come – just kidding. Let the young people have their fun. Anyway my wife's cooking. I better head home soon too or else she'll be angry,' he said and waved at them. Taking that as their signal, they said goodbye and hurried out.

Walking side by side Nitani said, 'Hey,' scrunching up his face. 'You make your feelings too obvious. Fuji's one of those guys who never says yes to a spontaneous drink so he was never going to come along. Even if you don't like him, you don't have to let it show.'

Strangely pleased by his seemingly deliberately sneering tone, she replied, 'But I really don't like him,' in an intentionally childish way.

They went to a yakitori joint about ten minutes' walk from the office. It was run by a Vietnamese family, and even though it was a yakitori restaurant, the menu also had things like pho, banh mi and coconut juice on it, and they offered a coriander salad to each customer, which they would substitute with pineapple for those who hated coriander; it was fun the way they blended Japanese and Vietnamese food, and Oshio liked to go there now and then. For that matter, she'd even gone there with Ashikawa. Back when she'd just been hired, they'd gone there once to eat banh mi together at lunchtime. We should come back for a drink sometime, she'd said, but that had not yet come to pass.

They got draft beers and clinked their glasses, then ordered a selection of skewers. They ate the coriander salad as they waited. 'So did you invite me out for a reason? Or did you just want a drink?' Nitani asked bluntly. She liked that about him.

'I just wanted a drink. Since Ashikawa went home, I had all this work to do and, I dunno, it's a small thing, really, and I already dealt with it all, but I just kept thinking, if I hadn't had to do this I could've gone home at seven. So I thought I'd use the money I'll get for this overtime and go for a drink.'

'Oh, so you're paying?'

'Why not?'

'C'mon. I can't let you do that.' Nitani drank from his beer glass. He drank quickly, as always.

'Don't you ever think, just take a paracetamol?'

'Is this about Ashikawa?'

The yakitori had arrived. 'Mind if I just eat it straight off the skewer?' he asked as he reached for the plate. She grabbed one of the sauce-covered skewers too, and blew on it.

'She says she has a migraine and has to go home, so, I mean, I get migraines too, you know. Right before it starts raining or whatever I always get a headache, so I keep drugs in my desk drawer at work. If I went home every time I have a fucking headache I'd never get any work done. But nobody ever suggests she take something for it.'

'I mean, you can't just say, "I don't care if your head hurts, you can't go home," not anymore.'

'But they think it, I'm sure. Everyone does.'

'Well, maybe.'

Nitani also had to help out with some bits and pieces of Ashikawa's unfinished work. How many calls had he had to make to suppliers when they hadn't received an invoice? It wasn't a big job, but having to do it frequently wore on him. He ought to have checked each purchase order to see if an invoice really hadn't been submitted and when it was supposed to have been submitted, but that was a hassle and none of this was his job in the first place, so he called them, made some apologetic small talk, and then made a note about when the invoices would come. Doing that for three or four suppliers took at least an hour.

Working overtime to cover for someone else was not quite the same as when it was your work. What was different was the way it made you feel. Not physically, mentally, you might think, but that was kind of physical too. A heaviness from the rear of your shoulders towards your back. The heaviness went downwards, to your hips, then around the front to linger where the fat gathered around your abdomen. Nitani took another bite of chicken. Am I unhappy, he wondered. He imagined his life working there for another, what, forty years. How he might be moved to another branch in that time, but wherever he went there'd be someone like Ashikawa there; how he'd have to work with them, day in, day out; how many more days, how many more hours' worth of work he would have to shoulder for someone else.

If you're not feeling well you should go home and let people who are well do the work instead, is what the boss said, but then that was surely a rule meant to be used only a limited number of times and only in the spirit of give-and-take. In the long run it's people who buckle down and people who are capable who make the world go around. The world. This one. The world we live in, within our reach.

'Oh God, I want a promotion.'

'Yeah?' Nitani said, with a startled look on his face.

'Yeah, I mean, I feel like, if I'm going to have to keep working like this I at least want a better job title for it.'

But a promotion would put her into a managerial position, and once you're in a managerial role then you have to manage people, and then she could definitely never tell someone who was suffering from a migraine to take some pills and do their work. It would come with extra responsibility. She wouldn't be able to say something like that at work nor, due to her position, would she be able to say it at after-work drinks like this.

'You wanna bully her because you can't say all this stuff to her? Or are you already doing it?'

'I'm doing it. Less bullying than just, you know, being normal.'

'What do you mean?'

'Everyone else is too nice to her, right? So I act normally. I ask a part-timer to sort out old documents instead of her, but then I ask Ashikawa to do things that employees ought to do, like handling disputes with suppliers and contract negotiations. Though to put it bluntly, I'd be better off asking someone like Harada who's been working here part-time for a long time to do that stuff too.'

It was office policy not to make Ashikawa do anything that might be a little too much for her. An unwritten and unspoken policy, but one that everyone had picked up on regardless. And she was just quietly breaking it. 'Here, you take this.' And Ashikawa would nod, looking slightly uncomfortable, and say, 'Sure.' There was something so affecting about her eyelids twitching anxiously that it almost made Oshio want to help her. She was pathetic and cute.

Oshio was happy hating her. Because the more endearing something pathetic was, the more power it held over you. It annoyed her that she had to be a bad guy like this. Why did people who were incapable of doing their jobs, who pushed their work off onto their co-workers, get to act like victims? And apparently Nitani and Ashikawa were going out. Harada had whispered the news to her like a warning, one day when it was just the two of them in the bathroom. It was none of her business. Harada was always, always trying to act like she and she alone truly represented the kindness of humanity, and all the while all she cared about was being nice to people who were easy to protect – it made Oshio sick.

'I'd like to hang out at your place sometime,' she said, as Nitani meaninglessly picked up his empty glass. The water droplets clinging to the side of the glass dripped down, forming a large drop, which inscribed a semicircle at the bottom of the glass before falling down. Nitani toyed with the small puddle on the table with his forefinger.

'Sure, but just so you know, I don't sleep with people I work with.'

'No office romances for you, then?'

'I mean, doesn't it seem somehow tainted? Finding love through the filter of work.'

Oshio smiled slightly. He thinks nobody knows.

'I get it, kinda.'

'"Kinda." What do you mean?'

'Because you'd have to hear other people's opinions whether you want to or not, and it's just different, I guess, because the question's always there: did you choose your partner purely based on your own judgement? Even if the other person's really nice, if they suck at work or something, then I'd hate that. That kind of thing, right?'

'Maybe.'

She entwined her pointer finger around Nitani's. His finger was damp to the knuckle. She'd wrapped her finger around his to transfer the water to hers, but it was drying little by little as she held it. Then I'll just let it dry like this, all of it, she thought, but Nitani murmured, 'Oh, uh,' and wiped his fingers and hers off with his napkin. It had brown marks on it from the yakitori sauce. Ashikawa's face appeared in her mind, though it had nothing to do with the stains.

'You really like books, huh?' I said, as soon as I walked into his flat; Nitani looked surprised and wary.

'How can you tell?' he frowned. Oh, I don't know, because there were stacks of paperbacks lined up underneath the windows. I just pointed and said, 'See?' Each stack had about thirty books in it, covers facing up, in a row along the wall as if they were holding each other up. On top of the books were a box of tissues, an open laptop, the remote control for the AC unit, a stack of loyalty and membership cards, cans of tuna and mackerel, and more. It'd be a pain in the ass if you took one of the books underneath out to read because you'd throw off the whole balance of the arrangement.

'No hardbacks,' I said, and Nitani furrowed his brows.

'They're expensive,' he said in a quiet voice, on his way to letting his guard down.

It was a simple flat. A studio with a separate kitchen, meant for living alone. The same floor plan as my place. A narrow kitchen just inside the entrance, with a toilet and bathroom directly opposite, and a thirteen-square metre room in the back. The bed, against the wall on the right, was a mess, left as it was when he'd got out of it. Next to the bed was one low table, small enough to be covered as soon as a meal for one was put on it. On top was a phone charger. That was all the furniture he had; I looked around and saw a closet door, closed, on the wall next to the kitchen.

I set my bag down and squatted down in front of the main tower. Lots of books by contemporary authors. Some by people who had won big prizes, others by people whose names I'd never even heard of.

'Do you like books too?'

'Mm, yeah, sorta.'

'What a weird answer.'

'I do like books but I don't keep up with things. At the moment I only read like one book a month. One of my friends from cheerleading in high school – she loved books so much she was in the literature club too. She read all the time, and she knew everything, so I feel like, compared to her I couldn't say I like books.'

'I mean, you don't need to compare yourself to anyone else. If you come over to my house and your eyes immediately go to my books, and you even sit down in front of them to look at them, then I think you like books.'

As Nitani spoke, he got two cans of beer out of his refrigerator. So we're drinking more – and beer? I was appalled but I still took the can; we cracked open our beers at the same time.

'I wasn't interested in them because I like books; I wanted to look at them because I want to know more about you. I was curious about what kind of books you read. So that's why I don't really think I should say I like books.'

'You're weirdly serious.'

So he's just going to ignore the part where I said I wanted to know more about him, I thought, frustrated, but as I considered it, I wasn't sure whether I actually liked Nitani or just wanted to seduce him. All the relationships I'd had thus far, I didn't know if I'd really loved them either; I'd held their hands because it seemed like I could, I'd kissed them because they seemed kissable, the vibe had been right so we'd slept together, and as a result we'd started going out and just kept on seeing each other, so maybe this was just the same. I was always the one who created the vibe, rather than being swept up in it. It was easy to do. And because it was easy to create, it was easy to change, too.

Nitani seemed to be trying to slow things down, not by putting his hand out to reduce the momentum but by putting the stacks of paperback books piled up along the wall in front like a dam. If that's how he wants it, I can make it work. Building a relationship without sex might be better, I might be more comfortable that way, I suddenly realised, and my heart began beating faster.

I made up my mind that this drink would be my last of the night, and after I finished it, I'd drink the tea I'd bought at the convenience store earlier, then call a taxi and go home; barely realising what I was doing, I took a sip from the can I held in my hand. As I did, I met Nitani's eyes. I felt a bad premonition in his colourless eyes, and though I tried to open my mouth to speak first, I couldn't because of the beer sliding down my throat.

'So are we going to do it?'

If you're going to say a line like that, your face ought to match it.

The serious look of a man suppressing the sexual desire that's arising in him. I wanted that fake seriousness. Nitani let the words lie there and turned his gaze to the books lined up against the wall. I had no idea what he was thinking. He didn't look like he wanted to fuck. Even if I said, no way, it didn't seem like it would hurt him, nor would it exactly put him at ease; it felt as if his heart just wasn't in it, as if he was evading things. His heart wasn't in it. Then where was it, I wondered. As I pondered this, I understood why I'd been attracted to the books. To bring our bodies together.

Contrary to expectations, Nitani's touch was gentle. I'd imagined he'd be more perfunctory, his heart not really in it, but his hands were gentle as they touched my skin, and his every movement was predicated on my response. I liked how polite, almost cowardly, he was. I was the one who had to get rough. I sank my teeth into his neck and he yelped, 'Ow!' I was frightened by the flatness of his voice. My hands, which had been wrapped around his naked back, dropped to his hips, and when I touched his crotch, it was certainly warm and hard, but his voice had been so cold.

Suddenly, I thought: leaving things here might be just right, and I let go of him. Nitani seemed to understand immediately; he lifted his hands, which had been roaming all over my body, and asked, 'You wanna stop?' I nodded. He slipped out of the covers.

I was lying on his bed, spaced out, when he asked me, 'You want some ramen?' He'd put a T-shirt on without me noticing.

'Now? Are you going to have some? You'll gain weight.'

I shook my hand to say no as I sat up. Nitani took one cup noodle from the stacks of them on top of his refrigerator, put tap water in a pan and put it on the hob. The lower half of his body, clad just in underwear, was defenceless and thin. So those are the legs I was just between, I thought, turning my attention next to my own body, and as I started to get up to put on my clothes, Nitani said, 'That's a no.' It was a clear declaration. For a moment, I thought he was talking about sleeping with me, but when I looked over at him, I realised he was about to put the cup noodle back on top of the fridge. He'd already torn off the outer packaging and put it in the rubbish. The packaging is definitely something we made at work, I thought, but I didn't bring it up.

'Changed your mind?'

'Yeah. I thought I wanted to eat, but then I remembered that I had bar food for dinner tonight. 'Cause we ate coriander or pineapple or whatever, something in my head glitched, and I felt like I'd eaten something proper at home.'

So he didn't decide not to eat it because he was worried about the calories. I wanted to dig into the details more, but I had just put on my bra and I was pulling my breasts together from the sides to push them into it, so all I could do was mutter, 'Oh?' I turned away from Nitani and put on my clothes, which were scattered on the floor. I wanted to have a shower. Tomorrow's a workday. I looked at my phone and saw it was time for the radio programme I always listened to in bed.

'I boiled some water,' Nitani said, making tea so as not to waste it. He set two mugs on the low table. A bag of black tea floated in each of them.

'I usually make two cups from one bag at home.'

'Me too, normally. I leave the bag in and make three

or four cups for myself like that. I thought I'd do things properly today.'

'Very hospitable of you.'

'What'd you major in, Oshio?' Nitani abruptly changed the subject.

'Tourism. Why ask now, all of a sudden?'

'What do you do when you study tourism?'

'We thought about regional development and made pamphlets about tourist destinations. For our graduation project, my seminar group, about twenty of us, spent a few weeks in turns, over two years, on an island in the Inland Sea that only has about one hundred residents, and while we lived there we created new tourism resources and put them out.'

'Huh. That actually sounds kind of productive.'

It sounded like praise but his tone felt somehow poisonous. To neutralise it I immediately continued talking.

'I mean, I'm from the countryside in Kyushu, so it felt kind of contradictory to overlook where I'm from and focus on developing tourism somewhere else rural, personally. So I guess that's why. It was meaningful and fulfilling but I couldn't digest it, so I didn't go into the field. Most of my classmates got jobs in tourism, though. Some of them even stayed there, in the Inland Sea.'

Nitani picked up the string of his teabag, raising and dunking it.

'You majored in economics, right?'

I remembered hearing him talking to someone at his welcome drinks and thinking that sounded just like him. Nitani took out his teabag and mine, wrapped them in a tissue and threw them away.

'I wanted to study literature but everyone kept saying I'd never get a job if I did because I'm a guy, so I thought maybe they were right, and I liked reading, but I didn't know if I really did want to do any research, so I went with economics instead. I didn't especially want to do economics research either, but I managed to graduate without doing it.'

I picked up one of the mugs but it was too hot to drink. I pulled it towards myself. As if assuming responsibility for the steam.

'The girl I was dating at the time didn't read novels at all, but she went into the literature department and she said, sure enough, it was all girls, so I felt like I'd made the right decision, but when I went over to her place she had books on literary history and theory on her shelf, books she said she'd had to buy because they were on the designated reading list, and she had more and more novels too, ones she'd had to buy for class, all lined up on this bookshelf built into the head of her bed. When

I was on top, when we were having sex, these books were above her head and I couldn't help but look at them, right? And I could see my sweat flying off, onto these books, soaking into the top edge of them, just a few drops so they'd dry without wrinkling, and she was facing the ceiling so she never noticed. I'd be the only one thinking about how my sweat was on them even after it dried. By our second year in uni, when she had so many books that the built-in bookshelf was no longer enough and she had towers of books stacked up on the floor, I started to think, you know, I really should've studied literature, and then I started to hate her, too. When I think about it now, I think I just hated myself, but at the time I was so irritated I blamed it on her: like, look at this fucking nerd buying all her textbooks, and so that's why we broke up.'

When I asked him if he was drunk, he said, 'I don't get drunk very much,' and took a gulp of his tea. Thinking he must be the kind of person who can handle hot things, I put my lips to my mug and was surprised it was drinkable.

When all but a fifth of my tea was gone and it had gone lukewarm, I called a taxi and went home. In the back of the cab, I came to the conclusion that the girl Nitani had dated when he was in university must have been like Ashikawa somehow. Then, I wondered for a moment if I'd done the wrong thing. But I hadn't. Not going through with it was the right thing to do. And I probably won't have sex with Nitani in the future either. So now we can be friends, with no hesitation.

Ashikawa was holding out muffins.

'I'm sorry about yesterday. Sometimes I have headaches so bad that painkillers just don't do anything. When I got home I took some more drugs and went to bed, and that helped, so I made these. Have one, if you like. Thank you for covering for me.'

Nitani went to grab one of the fist-sized cakes, wrapped in translucent plastic with pink flowers printed on it and tied with a light green ribbon, with one hand, but then realised that might seem rude, so he took his other hand from his keyboard and took it with both hands instead. 'Thank you,' he said. And: 'You didn't have to do that.'

The words had come from Nitani's mouth but they were ones he'd heard the boss and several superiors say before Ashikawa had made her way to his desk. A few had already started to eat. 'Oh, that's good,' Fuji said, his voice filled with genuine emotion. Ashikawa turned towards him and giggled with a smile.

'I think I'll save mine for after lunch,' Nitani said, setting it behind the phone on the far left of his desk. Ashikawa nodded deeply in understanding, took out the next muffin from the paper bag hanging from her right arm, and went over to Oshio's desk. Nitani's eyes met with Oshio's over Ashikawa's back for a moment. Her face was prepared with a perfect smile to welcome Ashikawa.

When Ashikawa apologised for going home early yesterday with her practised lines and handed her a muffin, Oshio said, 'Wo-ow, I couldn't make something like this. Looks great,' loud enough so that others could hear.

'There just aren't many girls these days who can bake,' said Fuji.

'That's so true. I've lived on my own since university so I can cook but I can't bake. I don't have the time,' Oshio said, then looked at Ashikawa and added, 'Really amazing.'

'It's not hard at all. Nothing amazing about it, really – just something simple I like to make sometimes.'

Ashikawa handed out muffins to all of the part-timers, and when she'd finished passing them around to everyone, she placed one on her own desk. She folded the empty paper bag and put it in her drawer. A sweet smell spread throughout the room; people here and there offered words of praise. When he looked over at Oshio's desk, the muffin was still there in its wrapping. Unlike Nitani's, which was sitting close to the edge of his desk, hers was sitting right in front of the computer. Her face was still smiling. She seemed to notice Nitani's gaze, but she did not meet it. He felt the need to pee and stood up from his chair.

Once he was out of the bathroom, he took out his phone to look at it as he walked down the short hallway and saw that he had a text.

'Anyone read the book that won the Booksellers' Prize?'

It was from a group chat for one of his seminars at uni. You could take a seminar of your choosing outside of your department only in your third year, as an elective and not a graduation requirement, but there was a literature class on the list so he'd taken it. They'd only seen each other every week for a year, but their group chat was still going, six years after graduation.

'Haven't read it. Any good?'

As he was looking at the screen, an almost-immediate reply came in from another member, who said: 'Pretty good! I thought it might win!'

Nitani had not read the book, nor had he known that it had won the Booksellers' Prize. But I did know the title and author's name, he thought with competitive pride. He didn't want his phone to keep on vibrating, so he turned notifications off and put his phone back into his breast pocket. Nitani hadn't said a word in this group chat, where everyone talked about books regularly, for a long time. He read every message. For a while he had been wondering when someone would remove him from the group, but it hadn't happened yet. With or without him, they would all continue to talk about books to their hearts' content.

If you like books, you should keep it as a hobby, like this chat. Nobody else in the group chat had majored in literature either. They'd done economics, law, engineering, and after graduation they'd gone into industries that had nothing to do with literature; it was just something they liked, so they kept up with it. Nitani, too, thought this was normal. But then whenever he worked with someone who had studied literature he would lose his shit, thinking: I chose economics because I thought it'd help me get a job, but then I keep running into people who did literature, the same age as me, or older or younger. When I chose what to do at uni when I was a teenager, I chose an easier life over what I actually wanted, he had thought over and over, though it was an exaggeration. Each time, he felt unable to accept the idea that it was enough just to like books. He felt like there were some things more important than your preferences, and that if you only paid attention to what you liked, then you might overlook them, or at least he hoped that was the case.

In the hallway where he had stopped, he saw an article from the company newsletter that had been put up on the wall, showcasing the new company building in

Okayama. The caption 'See the Wonders of the Roof Garden' irritated him. Not 'the wonderful roof garden', but the *wonders* of the roof garden. What fucking wonders? Though he was just quibbling, the anger burned in him, welling up from his stomach.

He went back to his desk and took another look over the materials for a meeting that Ashikawa had left when she'd gone home early the day before; he redid a few graphs and changed the order of the items on the agenda. He understood exactly what Oshio had been saying yesterday. It was a feeling he knew well. Neither of them wanted people to think they were weak. More than that, they didn't want people to think they were incompetent. They wanted people to think they were as good as anyone else, if not better. For everyone to think that. It wasn't just helpless people-pleasing. Who wants to prepare handouts for a meeting? Does anyone live just to make graphs? If everyone just went about life choosing to do what they wanted, what they could do easily, what they were comfortable with, then nothing would ever happen. If someone doesn't do the stuff no one wants to do, even though it's hard, then the work won't get done. And if the work doesn't get done then the company will go bust. And to say that such a company *should* go bust, well, that was just silly. Nitani agreed with all of that. But he also thought that the pale colour of Ashikawa's face as she said, 'I have a headache so I'm going home,' as if it were the most natural thing in the world, was also true.

His sense of smell, which had been reset by stepping out into the hallway for a little bit, leapt at the sweet scent wafting through the room. 'Really good, thank you.' People were *still* saying stuff like that. He reached for the phone to make a call, and his fingertips touched the muffin sitting behind it.

'I'm glad everyone liked them.'

Since then, Ashikawa had started occasionally bringing in homemade treats.

On Friday nights, Ashikawa came over to Nitani's place. When she arrived she changed into a long, soft dress that she used as loungewear, then said, 'Well, I'm going to make dinner now,' and went to the kitchen. Each time, Nitani choked back the words, 'Why don't we just get a takeaway?' Cucumber and whitebait marinated in vinegar, soy sauce and mirin. Fried chicken drizzled with a ginger-garlic sauce. Miso soup with fried aubergine. With just a single burner, Ashikawa cooked multiple dishes skilfully, even cleaning up as she went. At first Nitani had tried to help, but when she said, 'You're actually just getting in my way,' he'd taken her seriously, so instead he retreated and sat on the bed, listening to the clattering of dishes.

About an hour later, Ashikawa shouted, 'Can you get out the beer and chopsticks?' He quit the game he'd been playing on his phone in the middle of a battle and stood up. Behind the darkened screen of his phone, now lying on the bed, Nitani's warriors, in battle against someone else's out there in the world, had lost their commander, and would probably lose because they'd have to send out auto-generated basic soldiers with only one damage, he imagined.

He put two cans of beer, two pairs of chopsticks, and a pack of pickled plums he'd taken out of the refrigerator on the low table, and he thought: I'd be good with just this, really. Just pickled plums and beer. And if we need something else, then there's microwavable rice, and cup noodles. If you feel like you need to eat something for your health, then the convenience store sells salads and grilled fish. Ashikawa brought the food over. The plates that wouldn't fit on the table were placed on top of a cardboard box that had contained some leather shoes he'd bought online.

They both put their hands together at the same time then started eating. Nitani picked up a slice of cucumber and said, 'Mmm.' He picked up a piece of fried chicken and said, 'That's good.' He slurped some miso soup and said, 'Yum.'

They finished eating in about fifteen minutes. The food that she'd spent about an hour making, from the moment she'd got in from work, was gone in just fifteen minutes. You ate three times a day, and having to do that every day was seriously exhausting. Which was why Nitani thought that since the supermarkets and convenience stores had all this food that they'd made there, there was no sense in going to all the trouble of making it yourself. He kept this thought to himself and instead said, 'Mmm.' It exhausted him to have to feel that everything he ate to give himself the energy to move and think was delicious, to have to show that to Ashikawa in words.

Putting her chopsticks down with a sigh, Ashikawa stood up, opened the refrigerator, and said, 'There's dessert too,' pulling out a plastic container filled with bite-sized chunks of watermelon.

While the shopkeeper, clad in traditional workwear, was away from where they sat, Nitani whispered, 'If we're just going to eat oden, we should've bought it at a convenience store and eaten it at home. We fucked up.'

'No way,' I said. 'Convenience store oden is good but it's no match for a proper one from an oden shop. Look, they have tomato oden, asparagus, even – you don't get that in a convenience store, and the beef tendon is practically falling apart.'

The oden place, tucked away in a residential area about ten minutes' walk from Nitani's building, was located on the ground floor of an old house that was plain, not especially quaint. It was a small restaurant with only one table for four and a six-seat counter running along where the oden was cooked. The breeze rattled the windows, lukewarm air sneaking inside with each gust. The shop was run solely by its elderly owner. The place was almost empty, perhaps because it was located far from the station, or perhaps because few people wanted to eat oden in the middle of the summer. Other than us, sitting close together on the far-right side of the counter, there was only one other customer, a man sitting at the other end of the counter near the door, with his shirt sleeves rolled up, drinking on his own.

The oden was rich and delicious. The Kansai-style dashi broth had a gentle taste and a light golden colour, just the sip of it I got as I ate a piece of lotus root was not enough – it made me want to put my lips right to the bowl and slurp it up. All those new variations are good, but the classics are always the best, I thought, as I picked up a piece of fishcake.

'Oshio, are you one of those people that's into food?'

Well, you're one of those people who asks weird questions, I thought, as I turned to look at him.

'Who doesn't like good food?'

Nitani laughed darkly.

'I hate the idea of arranging my life around eating food.'

The owner asked if we wanted anything to drink. Nitani and I were just about to finish our second beer. Nitani ordered a third, and I ordered a glass of sake.

'Some days I want to eat oden, sure, but going to an oden shop makes me feel like my time and actions are controlled by food. Hate it. If they sell it in a convenience store then that's good enough for me. That's how I feel.'

'We didn't come here especially to eat oden – we were just wandering around thinking about where we should eat tonight, and you said, "Oh yeah, I think there's an oden place over there," so what's wrong with that? That's not being controlled by food, like you said, is it?'

Nitani put his hand to his chin, still holding his chopsticks, and thought for a while. When I had finished eating a piece of chikuwa fish sausage, which gushed with juice when I bit into it, he said, 'I think we were safe today.' I could sense from the way he said 'safe' that this was a real fixation of his so, rather than drag it out any longer, I decided to dig in a little further.

'I like good food, in the sense that I feel lucky if I get to eat it, but it's not the focus of my life. I don't understand people who travel a long way by car or train just to get something to eat. I think that's pretty stupid. But

I like to eat good food at places I can walk to from my house, like this. After all, even if it's a hassle, you still have to eat every day. That's why I think, rather than going to the supermarket and spending time thinking about what to have, cutting and cooking, and then, in the blink of an eye, eating what I've made, I'd rather go somewhere like this place, where I can pay for food made by a professional, sit and talk, and then eat what I'm served,' I said, then took a deep breath. 'Don't you think so too, Nitani?'

As I spoke, the look on Nitani's face gradually softened, and I could not stop myself from talking; the words tumbled out easily, but they were mostly lies. Cooking is a pain in the arse but eating out every day costs a lot and it makes you feel sick. On my days off, I take the train into Tokyo and go to restaurants that are known for their excellent set lunches, and I've also been known to take little foodie trips too. During the Golden Week string of bank holidays this year, four of my friends from cheerleading and I had just done a tour of Shinshu-style soba restaurants.

I looked at Nitani as he nodded in agreement while he drank his beer, then put his glass down and said, 'I get it,' and I wondered what on earth he hated so much about it all. Good food, cooking. I felt like they were all the *result* of whatever it was he hated.

Nitani had eaten the oden, and the yakitori the other

day, and the bar food before that, and said it was all good, like anyone would, but that reaction didn't seem like one that actually came from the bottom of his heart. He liked beer and drank a lot of it, but I wasn't sure whether that was because he really thought it was good. Maybe he just had to drink. You eat food every day. You eat it because if you don't, you'll die.

'I know you think it's a hassle to eat but what is it you don't like about it? That you have to do it?'

I looked at him and his eyes were dark. 'I hate everything around it,' he said. I had two feelings within me: the desire to understand him and for his eyes to remain as they were.

'"Around"?' I asked. 'Don't you worry that people will think you're being childish? I feel like people who will eat anything and say it's good are considered more mature, more advanced, even.'

Nitani poked at the kon'nyaku jelly in his bowl with his chopsticks.

'You know, if someone buys trendy clothes each season then throws them away when they're still wearable, people wouldn't say, "Oh, how horrible, there are people in this world who are so poor they only have rags to wear," but they're quick to say that about food. Even if it's not as extreme as throwing away a whole meal you didn't touch – if you just leave two mouthfuls of rice in your bowl or declare you don't really like eating, then right away, people start talking about you behind your back, like the heavens are going to punish you, that kind of thing. Nitani,' I said, making eye contact as I said his name. 'Look around the world. How many people out there are going hungry? You can say all that because you were born in a rich country, where you don't have to worry about where your next meal is coming from.'

Nitani burst into laughter.

'You sound just like Harada.'

'Oh, you liked my impression?'

'It's great – just like her,' Nitani said, still laughing. 'Too good. A perfectly guilt-inducing way of speaking.' He reached for his glass. I imagined Ashikawa might say the thing about how many people are going hungry in the world too, but she would say it to show how sad it made her, not to criticise someone else.

'Ashikawa sure seems to like good food.'

Right in front of where Nitani was looking was the oden pot, with potatoes and kon'nyaku submerged in its golden broth. Ashikawa would've taken one look at that and squealed, 'That. Looks. So. Good!' really drawing out each word. Just imagining it gave me a heavy feeling in my chest.

'Yeah. That girl does things the way you're supposed to.'

'The way you say it makes it sound like we don't.'

I was happy to hear him call her 'that girl' so coldly; I pushed his right arm with my left. Nitani picked up his half-empty glass, went to drink from it and stopped. 'Gimme a sip,' he said, picking up my glass of sake. He threw it back, to my surprise, and I said I didn't think he liked sake, to which he said, 'No, I'll drink anything.' He held up the transparent sake glass in his right hand. 'This is good.' Transparent is transparent whether you hold it up to the light or not, so what was he trying to see? It was funny to me. And that statement of how good it was had seemed earnest, which became funnier the more I thought about it, and I laughed.

Just a few minutes after stepping out of the air-conditioned office, Nitani had begun to sweat profusely. The sun was about to start setting, but the heat emanating from the lingering memory of midday was enough to make him perspire. He had gone to the vending machine to buy a coffee but wound up buying carbonated water instead. Only the palms of his hands, holding the plastic bottle, felt any escape from the heat. As he turned around to go back to work, he saw Ashikawa standing just outside the wall separating the office from the main road. She noticed him, smiled harder, and raised her hand. As he approached, Ashikawa said excitedly,

'Oh, perfect! My brother's almost here with Mukosuke. In the car. You want to see him?'

'Oh, really? Yeah, I'd like to pet him.'

Excited to hear that a dog was coming, Nitani came out through the main gate. Not long after, an estate car pulled up. The passenger window opened and a man who looked a few years younger than Nitani said, 'Hello,' craning his neck from the driver's seat.

'I work with your sister. Nice to meet you,' Nitani said, returning the greeting, and peered into the car. Mukosuke was in the back seat. He had brown fur, black only around his nose, and gentle features. Ashikawa slowly opened the door a little so that Mukosuke wouldn't leap out. She tried to pick the dog up, but in his excitement Mukosuke was barking and running back and forth along the seat; he would not calm down, so she had a hard time.

'I don't want him to jump out so I'll just say hello from here,' Nitani said.

Ashikawa said, 'I'm going to get in. Then, I'll hold him and put his head out the window, and then you can pet him.' She quickly got in from the other side. As she did, her younger brother turned to him.

'I hope my sister's not too bad to work with.'

'Not at all. I just got transferred to this branch in the spring, and she's taken me under her wing. I really owe her.'

'Under her wing? My sister?'

Her brother sounded surprised. Nitani sensed the contempt contained within. Ashikawa opened the back window. She put Mukosuke on her lap and held him from behind to keep him from jumping out. Mukosuke looked up at Nitani, as excited as ever. Even the black spots on his lolling tongue were cute. When Nitani approached with his palm facing up, Mukosuke pressed his wet nose against it and smelled him. He rubbed under the dog's chin with his now-damp hand, stroked his cheek, petted his head. The warmth of the dog and its beastly dampness, which he had not felt for a long time, made him happy.

Her brother was wearing a suit. Seemingly on his way home from work. 'Are you taking Mukosuke out now?' Nitani asked, tilting his head. It was too close to sunset for a long walk, so Nitani wondered if he was taking him to the vet or something.

'He's taking him to a kennel,' Ashikawa answered instead of her brother. 'Actually my brother is getting married. His fiancée's house is far away, so they decided to have both families meet there. So, early tomorrow morning, my parents and brother are going away for two days and one night.'

'Oh, I see. Well, congratulations.' Nitani turned to her younger brother and bowed. Her brother said thank you and bowed slightly in response. 'Right, so while you're away the kennel will take care of him,' Nitani said, stroking the dog's head.

'And I'll take care of the house,' Ashikawa said. Nitani lifted his hand from the dog's fur and looked at Ashikawa's face. 'This time is just for the parents to meet. His fiancée's siblings don't live in the area anymore either so all the rest of us will have to meet for the first time at the wedding. So I'll be home alone.' She sighed. 'I wanted to go on a trip too,' she said, looking frustrated.

'Then why are you taking him to the kennel?' Nitani asked, and her younger brother sighed exaggeratedly. It almost sounded like a laugh.

'She can't take care of Mukosuke on her own. She can't feed him or take him for a walk alone either. Mukosuke obeys me or Mum and Dad, but he won't listen to her at all.'

Ashikawa understandably puffed out her cheeks and made a face, then lightly punched her brother on the arm. Nitani wondered if she would say something, but all she did was groan. Mukosuke licked Nitani's hand.

We walked to the station and went into an okonomiyaki place. Colourful posters on the walls proclaimed, handwritten, that it was authentic because the owner was from Osaka. There were four tables with large, built-in steel griddles and six sunken-in low tables for sitting on the floor, also with their own built-in griddles; the restaurant was half full. I sat in a chair across the only free table from Nitani, ordered two draft beers from the waiter, who brought us warm handcloths, and opened the menu.

'Where'd you go over the Bon holidays?'

'Bon kinda sucked. I just stayed in Tokyo the whole time.'

'What sucked about it?'

'I've been invited to a high-school friend's wedding next month, and everyone else I know that's going was on the cheerleading team too, so we thought we'd do a cheer routine at the reception. It's going to be a surprise to the couple, but we'll get the groom to participate a little . . . Well, I wound up spending the whole holiday planning and practising for it.' Just remembering it made me sigh heavily.

'Oh, yeah, that does kind of suck. I haven't really seen too many cheer routines before but they're not like how people imagine cheerleaders, right? It's pretty tough, like a group gymnastics routine or something.'

'Yeah, those kind of cheerleaders don't really exist. What people imagine, that's more like a costume, or something like it. What cheer teams do at practice or matches, or at competitions, is more like cheer dance routines.'

'Sure.' Nitani nodded, as if he were au fait with all of this.

'A cheerleader . . . leads cheers, right? It sounds so simple. But cheerleading is pretty hard to do without a lot of practice, and it can be dangerous. Getting up on someone's shoulders, much less *standing up* on someone else's shoulders, doing three-tiered formations, the fan-shaped ones where you support each other with just your arm strength, marching in formation without messing it up, none of that is easy even if you used to do it a long time ago. That's why I didn't want to perform at the wedding in the first place.'

'But you got dragged into it.'

I nodded. The waiter brought over our beers. We ordered asparagus and pork jowl stir fry and a tofu steak. The waiter wrote down our orders, went back to the kitchen, and quickly brought back plates for us. He turned on the heat under the griddle and poured some oil, then began to cook the asparagus and pork jowl and, a little further away, the roughly cut tofu. The smell of the soy sauce burning on the tofu wafted. The waiter said to wait until the food was cooked through to eat, then left.

'Obviously pyramid routines were out, so we decided to form a line and do complicated upper-body movements, and I wound up only doing a small part, but trying to do moves with pom-poms in hand that look legit takes a lot of muscle in itself. Just getting the routine down takes a few practices, but to really get it sharp, it's not enough just to practise at home on your own.'

'You're from . . . I wanna say, Kyushu, right?'

'Fukuoka. Not Fukuoka City, rural Fukuoka.'

'Must be pretty hard to practise if your friends are all back home.'

'About half of them live around here now. A few are in Osaka or wherever. We practised in small groups, and the wedding is being held back home, so we're going to get together the day before . . . so, you know, it's not going to go very well.'

Nitani flipped the pork jowl and asparagus with the spatula. The sizzling started again.

'You take things pretty seriously, Oshio,' Nitani muttered, neither admiringly nor sarcastically; he appeared to have said it purely because he had thought it. 'It's not because you love cheer so much that you want to do it justice, right? It's that if you're going to do something, you want to do it well.'

I was a little taken aback. Nitani was exactly right. While I was thinking of what to say in response, Nitani got the waiter's attention and ordered another beer. 'Not a pint but a bottle, and two glasses, oh, and make it a big bottle,' he said, so I waited until the bottle of beer and frosty glasses had been brought over before speaking.

'I don't particularly care about cheerleading, but I do

take things seriously, and it's something I could do so I did it, you know? I did cheer until just before the summer of my third year of high school, so that's two years I was really actively doing it. Not many kids from my middle school were in my class in high school, and this girl I sat next to said she was going to try out for the cheer team so I went along with her. So that's how we both wound up joining the team, and practices were pretty tough, but then sports club practices are all pretty hardcore in their own ways, right? But I didn't really hate it either, so I just stuck with it until the end. That's all. Even though it's something I did in high school, now that I'm a real adult, people still say, "Oh, you were a *cheerleader*, no wonder you're so full of energy," which I kind of hate, so the idea made me grit my teeth, to do a cheer performance at a wedding.'

We'll never be able to perform at the same level after just a handful of practices like we did when we were in high school and practised every day, so the best we'll be able to do is something that'll appear like an imitation, and all we'll see reflected in the happy couple's eyes is that imitation, but they'll know they have to act like they're so impressed, and actually it might be worse if they really *are* impressed. Like, why the hell would you be. And yeah, we're friends, but I can't imagine still being so obsessed with something we did for just a couple of years.

'I'm not very good at quitting things. Just thinking about the whole kerfuffle of saying I'm quitting, and everyone else's reactions, it's overwhelming. It didn't really cross my mind when I thought we wouldn't meet up, but then practising every day is just so *tough*. Everyone else said the same thing so I thought we were all in it together. I only realised I was wrong after we aged out of the team. Everyone else talked about how they wanted to cheer more. And they all looked serious, saying they wanted us all to get up on stage together again, that they were going to do cheer in uni. No way did I feel like that. No fucking way. So I guess cheer wasn't really for me. I don't especially like cheering on or supporting people, but I'm good at it, and I knew that I could do it. It's a lot like work, actually. I mean, I guess I can keep working like this until I retire, but every day I hate it. Though I probably shouldn't be saying all of this to you, since we work together and you kind of outrank me. But everybody says it, don't they – "work sucks", right? So it's pretty normal. I hate it but I get up every day and I do my job, and I guess that's just how it's always going to be.'

'I don't actually hate it that much.'

'Are you serious?'

'Yeah. It's not like I have anything else to do.' Nitani grinned and I understood that he was joking.

'No, of course you do. There's lots of other stuff you

could do. Ughhh, this performance. I'm going to be at a wedding and I can't even drink until after we've done it!'

'And you eat at weddings too,' Nitani mumbled, a look of exasperation crossing his face. 'Pretty horrible that you can't even celebrate people without having to eat and drink while you're doing it.'

'Yeah,' I nodded, thinking that I should practise the routine again when I got home, even though I felt like I was starting to get drunk.

Nitani returned to his desk carrying the sample books of label colours and had just sat down in front of his computer when, out of the corner of his eye, he saw Oshio sigh. He was wondering if she was still hung up on the small mistake she'd made that morning when he saw Ashikawa come out of the kitchen and say to everyone, 'It's three o'clock – snack time, everyone?' It was then that Nitani understood the real meaning behind Oshio's sigh.

'I made a cake today.' Ashikawa pulled an armful of a paper box out from the refrigerator and carried it over. Some of the part-timers started talking about how it looked as if it had come from a bakery before any of them had seen the contents of the box yet. Ashikawa giggled and smiled, put the cake down on the meeting room table, and opened the sides of the box to take it out. It was a whole shortcake, decorated generously with pure white fresh cream and juicy fruits like satsuma and kiwi. In an instant the air turned sweet.

'Wow. Right?'

Fuji had turned to me to say the last part, so I said back, 'Yeah, it's amazing.' Some of the women part-timers were taking pictures of it with their phones.

Ashikawa hadn't stayed over last weekend. She said she'd had a nappe class on Saturday and then spent all day Sunday making a cake. This must've been what she had made.

'What does "nappe" mean?' Nitani had asked the previous weekend, while eating the salmon meuniere she had made. Her expression as she explained had been uncharacteristically proud.

'It's a technique where you evenly spread cream over a whole cake. No gaps, at a nice, uniform thickness, as if it were done by machine.'

If I want to eat a cake that looks like it was frosted by a machine, then I'd just buy one made in a factory, Nitani thought, but Ashikawa did not seem to feel the same. 'I'll learn it on Saturday and then make a cake on Sunday, and if it's a success then I'll bring it,' she trilled. Nitani knew that she did not mean she would bring it over to his place, though he thought she should have; instead, she would bring it into the office.

'Where's your class being held?'

'Jiyugaoka. It's a class but it's not at a cooking school or anything; it's in someone's house, but she's a really good cook, so she sometimes gets people together at her house and teaches these kind of little tricks. I saw some pictures on social media – her kitchen is really huge and so pretty.'

'Jiyugaoka? Isn't that in Tokyo? You're going all the way to Tokyo?' he asked, surprised, and Ashikawa simply nodded and continued talking.

'She actually has a full-time job somewhere in the financial district, and she makes this gorgeous-looking food every day even though she must be really busy at work, and on her days off she bakes too, and the pictures she uploads to social media are really popular, so I bet someday she'll write her own cookbook' – on and on she went, her eyes gleaming.

'Do you wish you were like her?' he asked.

Ashikawa suddenly stopped talking.

'Maybe,' she agreed quietly. Jeez, it doesn't take much for her to idolise someone, Nitani thought, feeling bored.

And now right in front of him was the cake Ashikawa had tried out her newly acquired nappe technique on.

'Excuse me, sorry, can everyone please line up here, take a piece and then move on?'

She cut the cake into pieces, putting one slice each on the plates meant for visitors. The knife she was using was a thin, pointed one with a serrated edge, meant for cutting cakes and bread without tearing either, something that Ashikawa had also brought in.

Everyone approached the entrance to the meeting space. Four slices of cake were already lined up on the table, but people seemed hesitant to be the first to take one; they said things like, 'Wow, you're amazing,' while waiting for her to finish cutting the entire cake. As Nitani joined at the edge of the circle, Oshio, who was standing closer to Ashikawa, two people separating them, said:

'Is there going to be enough for everyone?'

'Ooh, I dunno, OK, one, two, three . . .' Everyone started counting, but despite their apparent surprise, everyone looked unbothered; they had known there wasn't enough the moment they had lined up in front of the cake.

'Oh my gosh, you're right! I brought only one cake, not two, so I'll only be able to cut it into eighths at best. I'm sorry, there's only enough for eight people! Figure out amongst yourselves who's going to have a piece!'

Everyone started muttering, the mood clearly dampened. Fuji moaned, in all seriousness, 'But I really wanted some,' sounding just like a man who had decided he couldn't eat cake at all anymore, and the woman standing next to him laughed. This laughter seemed to cheer him up. 'I mean, if you'd asked, Ashikawa, I would've driven over to your house. Then you could have brought in two or even three cakes. See? So just let me know next time, all right?' he added. Ashikawa's eyes were still turned to the cake and the knife, but a smile began to appear quite obviously at the corners of her down-turned mouth.

'You're right, my mistake. I'll do just that next time!'

Around when they'd settled on deciding by rock paper scissors, a phone rang. It was the phone on Fuji's desk, but Oshio jumped from the *br* of the first *brring*, reaching out for the phone on the nearest desk. From the way she spoke it sounded like it was an enquiry from another branch. 'We certainly were able to handle things like that last year, however . . .' she continued, without deferring to Fuji. Then, receiver still held to her ear, she pointed with her empty hand, so everyone could see, at the cake, then waved to say 'bye'. Everyone around her nodded. Bad timing, someone said sympathetically.

'Another competitor down,' Fuji joked.

Nitani happened to look at his watch and saw it was 3:20. His next meeting was in forty minutes, so it was obviously too early to start preparing, but seeing that everyone except Oshio was still standing around and gabbing, he felt like the thick-battered deep-fried chicken from the convenience store bento he'd eaten for lunch was returning to its original form in his stomach. Deliberately, but in a way that he thought sounded natural, he sighed and muttered, 'Oh, right.' Then he said, 'Got a meeting coming up. I've got to go prepare for it, but you guys enjoy.' Once he'd started walking away, he added, 'Damn, that cake looked good, too.'

He met Fuji's eyes. He thought Fuji would make a remark like before.

'No, Nitani, you have to have some.'

He said it in a very clear tone. 'What?' Nitani said, sounding idiotic. He hastily closed his mouth, then opened it again and said, 'Sorry, what was that?' with a slight smile.

'C'mon, you know what I mean.'

His tone of voice was deeply suggestive, and some of the people around him, mainly part-timers, grinned and turned to look. What the hell, does everybody know somehow? Feeling everyone's gaze, even Oshio's, who was still on the phone, made his spine go cold. Ashikawa must have heard the whole exchange too, but she didn't even glance over; she was correcting the angle of a strawberry on top of a slice of cake. You're in on it too, he thought bitterly, but instead he said, intentionally idiotically, 'Haven't got a clue,' and felt like hurting himself. It was times like these when he wanted to die. He wanted to be able to throw it back in someone else's face, tell them how badly he wanted to get fucked up and then say: I'm dead, look, I'm dead, I told you this would happen.

In the end, Nitani wound up getting one of the eight pieces of cake, and he could not exactly say, under the surveillance of all those grins, that he would eat it later, nor did he want to eat the cake later and have everyone's eyes on him as he ate it alone; he had no choice but to eat it on the spot.

'It's so good, better than the ones you get from the store,' Fuji, who had weaselled his way into getting a slice, said loudly. The other winners also moaned little words of appreciation, each with an audible exclamation mark, one by one: 'Mm!' 'Yum!' 'Wow!' This was a matter of politeness.

The rules of politeness for eating homemade treats: you must talk loudly while eating. You must continually perform gratitude. You must say, 'This is so good,' when you take your first bite; once you've eaten half, ask about something you have no interest in, for example, 'Wow, how do you make a sauce like this?'; once you've finished, you must declare in a particularly satisfied-sounding voice, 'Gosh, that was good! Thank you!'

All that effort just because you were given a slice of cake. And why does nobody ever talk about it? So Nitani thought to himself, but when he lifted his fork, he said instead, 'This looks great, thank you,' and once he'd had a bite, he also said, 'Wow, this is so good,' though he ate the rest of it in silence.

The fresh cream filled his mouth. It penetrated to

the back of his teeth and into the space partitioned off by the gums above his molars. He bit into the satsuma and kiwi and crushed them. Juice gushed out. Wanting to narrow its range as much as possible, he lifted his chin up a little, tilting his head. Every time he chewed, it made a vulgar sound: *nghaa.* Fresh cream smeared on his tongue and fruit juice on top of it. The sponge rustled, touching here and there in his mouth. Some parts were soft and some were moist, but in the end they were all sodden with cream and fruit juices. Chew and grind. When he swallowed, an even sweeter, heavier smell rose from his throat into the back of his mouth and up to his nose.

Not so quickly that it would seem unnatural, he brought the fork up to his mouth, so as to appear as if he were savouring it but that it was so good that he might just eat the whole thing right away. If something is delicious you have to smile. And while you are eating, your mouth is full so you can't smile. He tried to smile with his eyes and cheeks, but his cheeks were always moving so they couldn't stay in place. In that case, of course, you just need to smile with your eyes, but the smell. The sweet, heavy smell violently forced its way out through his nose and hit his eyes. He tried to clench his stomach. If he clenched hard he stopped breathing for a second, and then the smell stopped too, but once he relaxed again it seemed several times sweeter than before.

When he had just one more bite left, he sensed someone staring; when he glanced around, he saw Oshio looking at him. Her face was perfectly expressionless, but when she locked eyes with Nitani, she said, 'That looks so good.'

'It really is,' Nitani said, putting the last bite in his already open mouth.

He took his plate and the one Fuji had used to the kitchen and washed them with the sponge and a little dish soap. Making sure no one was looking, he took a gulp of water, swished it around his mouth and spat it out in the sink. He wiped his mouth with the back of his hand. When he realised that everybody had said the cake was so delicious but nobody had said a thing about the nappe, or how wonderfully the cream had been applied, bile rose and he felt a little better.

Though it was October, it was still so hot that the walk just from the station to his house made his underwear damp with sweat. He was fed up with summer, wanted to know how much longer it would go on for, but after two days of continuous rain, it suddenly became cooler. Around that time, a large order had come in at work and suddenly things got hectic. Fuji had made a sour face, as if to say, geez, what a busy end of the year, though when Nitani had asked him if he thought they would manage to get it done in time, to confirm the schedule, Fuji spat out that he didn't want to think about anything to do with the period between New Year and early spring.

They could no longer go home on time, so each day, a little after the end of the day, Nitani would go to the kitchen, eat the onigiri or pastries that he had bought from the convenience store at lunchtime, and take a short break. Nothing else he could do about his hunger. After that, he would work until ten or eleven. Oshio kept some boiled eggs she made at home in the refrigerator and, when she got hungry, she drank a powdered soup she mixed up in a mug. Some people would go out to a nearby place to eat a beef bowl. It frustrated Nitani that he couldn't just quit eating even though he had so much work to do. Some people, like Fuji, got by on eating snacks, waiting until they got home to eat dinner, but Nitani couldn't understand it. He looked at them suspiciously, these people who would go to such lengths to have a proper meal.

Ashikawa usually went home between six and seven. Usually around quarter past six. If she stayed until seven for two or three days in a row, she would feel ill the next day and call in sick, so rather than having to deal with her being out, when it got to six o'clock, everyone would turn to her and say, 'Shouldn't you be heading home now?' Ashikawa would smile weakly, report on how she felt (for example, 'That headache's sort of still with me today') and then go home.

When Oshio sighed loudly at the sound of the door closing behind Ashikawa, Fuji said:

'Let it go. I'm sure you've heard stories about other companies where people get shouted at if they even think about calling in sick.'

As he spoke he waved his right hand back and forth, in a motion suggestive of scaring off flies, and Oshio sighed even louder in response.

'I brought this for today.'

Ashikawa smiled, holding out a golden-coloured peach tart. It was an individual tart, which she put on a light blue sheet of Japanese serving paper. The first thing that popped into his head was: you had time to make something like that on a *weekday*?

'That looks seriously amazing.'

Nitani looked at Ashikawa, the eyebrows on his face lowered. 'Wow,' he added in an excited voice. 'Thank you as always.'

Ashikawa smiled back, as if to say, no, no, thank *you*. Her hair swayed as she shook her head back and forth. She then went to hand a tart to the next person. Nitani said, in a voice loud enough for everyone around him to hear, 'I'm going to save this, as a reward for finishing work today.' He wrapped the whole thing, paper and all, in clingfilm, attached a sticky note with his name on top, and put it in the refrigerator.

Ashikawa left on time that day; Fuji and Oshio left around nine. I'm going to stay a little longer, Nitani said to them. Once he was alone, he took the tart out of the refrigerator.

He peeled the clingfilm off from where it had stuck to the peaches. It smelled both sweet and sour. The brown crust of the tart was hard, and underneath the peaches it was filled with a layer of custard. When Ashikawa had handed out the tarts everyone had said how incredible it was that she could make tarts by hand too. He thought, it must take a lot of effort to make the dough, put it in moulds and bake it, make the base of the tarts, spread the custard on them, put drained canned peaches on top, cool it in the refrigerator, carry it all to work without destroying any, then take them out just when everybody was starting to get tired and hand them out with a smile. He wondered why she would do all of that, but he knew that he'd only asked himself the question so he could conclude that she was a moron.

Once he was alone the air conditioning sounded loud to him. The lights were only on above his desk; a third of the room was dark. The darkness and silence that he had not noticed when he was concentrating on his computer screen enveloped him. Nitani placed the peach tart on his desk, between his body and the computer, extended his arms around it and typed up the minutes from today's meeting. Once he'd finished the last line, he moved the mouse with his right hand and scrolled through, scanning the document over quickly from top to bottom. Deciding to check for any little typos tomorrow, he saved the file and closed it.

He picked his hand up from the mouse and moved it straight over the tart, then dropped it.

A cold, sticky resistance met his hand, still held as if cradling his mouse. He forced his palm downward. His fingers curled, stretching up. The outline of the tart crumbled under his hand; he could feel fragments of it sticking in the custard. Soon after, a peach slipped between his fingers and light yellow cream spurted out. His skin felt moist and cool where the custard had reached. He raised his right hand.

With his left hand he pulled out a tissue and wiped his other, cream-covered hand. He put the used tissue over the crushed tart and put both in a plastic bag. Then, he turned off his computer and stood up.

As he walked down the hallway, he gripped the plastic bag in his hand, then squeezed the air out of it until it was flat, crumpled it into a ball and threw it in the bin. The large bin, waist-height, was empty, having apparently just been cleaned. The sound of the bag falling into it echoed in the darkened hallway.

He took the office key to the guard's room, then went out. The wind was cold. As he walked from the station towards his flat, he realised that he was hungry, and though it irritated him he knew it was unavoidable. When you're hungry you have to eat. There was one convenience store and one supermarket on his way home. As he walked, trying to decide which to go to, he felt dispirited.

I left the office with Nitani around midnight, and we went to a chain izakaya that stayed open until three. I had chicken nanban, a tomato salad, white rice and miso soup, and left after half an hour. Nitani only drank one beer, while I had oolong tea. Maybe it was because I was always so tired then, but having a beer made me feel sluggish. My body would get drunk before my mind did. If I knew I had to go to work the next day I couldn't drink. 'You're having a real dinner,' Nitani said, watching me drink my oolong tea; his face was tired too. It looked like it was covered with a grey filter. 'Is it still only Wednesday?' He sounded feeble.

When we left the bar and started walking towards the station, a cat crossed the road about two metres ahead of us. The big white cat quickly disappeared without giving us a single glance. Both Nitani and I followed the cat with our gaze, and though we continued walking without stopping or even mentioning it, I said, 'Oh, that reminds me.

'Now this happened before you came to our branch, but one time, Ashikawa and I were on our way back from a meeting with a client when we heard a cat crying. It was pretty intense, and the crying just kept going, so we got worried and tried to go towards the sound. We got to this quiet residential street, a bit away from the station, where there was a little stream, and when I looked down from the bridge, I saw the cat there crying, sitting in this hole in the riverbed, right next to the water. I say it was a hole, but it was like a square walled space, wide enough to fit a big refrigerator. No idea what it was for. The top edge was slightly above ground level. So the cat was at the bottom, surrounded by concrete walls on all sides. I think a cat would generally be able to jump that height, but the walls were vertical and the way that the cat was crying was not normal, so I guess it couldn't get out. Ashikawa was like, "Oh no, what should we do?" So the two of us went down to the water.'

It had been early autumn. The meeting had been with a small company selling organic vegetables who had wanted to switch their packaging from plastic to paper and change the design while they were at it. The man we met with, who was nearing retirement age, wasn't horrible towards Ashikawa or me, but he did say, in a reproachful tone, 'Pretty girls like you shouldn't be working.' Ashikawa mostly giggled, while I tried to explain the design; he kept interrupting me, and in the end I just had to listen to this man's stories about the good ol' days. I wondered if Fuji, who had sent us, knew that this would happen. I managed eventually to get an agreement out of him that the next meeting, to explain the design in a more detailed fashion, would take place at our offices. Ashikawa was delighted, which irritated me, because I felt like she was utterly clueless.

'So then what?' Nitani said.

'There were some stairs nearby, and so we went down to the riverbank. When we got close to the hole that the cat had fallen in, I saw that the concrete edge sticking up from the ground was about knee-high, and there was the cat, about two metres below. Seeing us there, the cat started meowing even louder. Ashikawa looked in next to me, and said, "What do we do?" Well, what else could we do? We had to save it. The cat would die otherwise. From up close you could see that the concrete walls were pretty nasty, covered in dirt and moss, and there were no rungs or anything, so it was impossible to get down there. I decided to lean in as far as I could and stretch my hand out. I couldn't reach anywhere near the cat, but the tip of my fingers managed to get about halfway down, so I thought maybe the cat might jump onto my arm. But the cat panicked, seeing a human there suddenly, and it turned away from me and started meowing even harder. I stayed like that for a little while, waiting for the cat to change its mind, but it didn't work, and the blood was starting to rush to my head, so I got up and sat down on the ground. Ashikawa said, "Wow, I could never do that in a skirt." I was wearing a skirt suit that day, so when I bent myself over that wall like that, it was, shall we say, not very ladylike. But only Ashikawa was there to see it, and the cat was more important anyway. Which is why I said, "Well, I know, but if we don't do something . . ." Then Ashikawa suggested we ask someone to come, and when I asked her who that someone might be, she said we should shout to any man walking down the street and ask him to help. That kind of, you know, threw me. I was bewildered. Her eyes were very sincere as she said it, and they seemed to almost twinkle, though maybe that's just because we were outside in broad daylight. That glimmer in her eyes made me feel like, wait, maybe I'm the crazy one here. But, no, because if we did get a man down there, would he even be able to get the cat? I had reached out to it and if the cat had felt like it, it could've jumped and come up, but that's not how the cat was, so then even if we got a man to help us it would make no difference, right? Now that I think about it, we should've called the police, or someone who could've brought a ladder or a net or something. But at the time I didn't think of that, for some reason. I thought I had to do something myself. So I said, "No, I don't want to. I'm wearing a skirt, and if we get a man down here to help, then I won't be able to bend over and reach out to the cat, so no." I was talking complete rubbish.'

I laughed hollowly and Nitani laughed along with me. He turned his eyes to the izakaya on the other side of the road from me, seeming to read the sign as he walked, so I thought he wasn't interested, but then he said, 'And then?'

'The rain started. The forecast had predicted rain that day. Heavy rain from the evening, it said. We'd talked about wanting to get back to the office before it started. I didn't know anything about the structure of this hole, but if there wasn't a drain in the bottom of it then it would fill up with water and the cat would drown, so in a panic I lowered my upper body into the hole and reached out again. The front of my suit had a grey stain on it where it pressed into the edge of the hole, but I didn't really care about that anymore. The cat was still trying to stay as far away from my hand as possible, and then, I had an idea, so I took everything out of my bag, just emptied it all out on the ground, and held that down into the hole. It was a large bag, one I could put A4 documents in, so when I stretched as far as I could, it almost went far enough to touch the cat. I thought maybe the cat wouldn't be as afraid of an object as of a human, I guess. Ashikawa kept asking me, "What's happening? Is everything OK?" I didn't say anything. I thought if I said something it would scare the cat. So I didn't say anything, just waited there patiently, for five or ten minutes, round about that, when suddenly the cat turned around, jumped in the bag, and then, like da-da-da, it jumped to my arm, then my shoulder, then to my back, and it was out of the hole. It felt light. By the time I got myself out of the hole, the cat was gone, and Ashikawa pointed to the road above us, saying that it ran that way. She opened her umbrella. It was a little compact one. White, with a violet floral pattern. What's strange is I can't remember what colour the cat was, but I remember her umbrella very clearly. The rain wasn't pouring down but it was sprinkling, and I had been leaning forward, so I was wet from my back to my waist. I thought that someone really ought to cover that hole up, so I looked up the address on the maps app on my phone so I could report it to city hall later, then we headed back to work. On the way back, Ashikawa kept going on about how much she really, really respected what I'd done. "Only a cheerleader would think of that," she even said. "I could never. I wish I was like you, Oshio." Wait, remember what I just said about the cat? I'm not totally sure but I think it was white too, actually. Never mind, it doesn't matter. Sorry for rambling. Somehow we always wind up talking about Ashikawa, huh. She's not here but she's all we talk about.'

Nitani, who had listened to my story while looking in the other direction, said, 'It's easy to talk about people you know.' I wondered if he wasn't going to say anything about the story about the cat, but when we got near to the station, he said, with a serious look on his face, 'I don't think strength or weakness has anything to do with saving a cat or not, so if someone said that to me, it'd bother me too.' I felt relieved by his words, but I also felt it was a little too simplistic, so I didn't say anything to Nitani; I just nodded silently. I suddenly thought, actually, I could just let it go. I'd thought that I hated Ashikawa because of all the unforgivable things she did, and while I did hate her, I also felt like I *could* forgive her, whatever she did. She was not beyond forgiveness for me. She was weak. She was weak, and that is why I hated her.

At the station I waved goodbye to Nitani. 'Take care,' he told me. On my way home, I thought about how Nitani was on the train right then, how the notification sound I'd heard from his phone before must've been a message from Ashikawa, and how he was reading it now, writing some kind of reply to her.

'Since I've been going home before everyone else,' Ashikawa said, explaining the increase in the frequency of her bringing in homemade treats. Nitani thought that because he had been working Saturdays too, and she could only see him on Sundays, that she had more time on her hands, but then he caught himself: what a weird way to think, that she only has free time because she's not seeing me. When we spend time together all we do is sit in my flat and watch movies or TV or just talk nonsense to each other, so if baking is her hobby then she really ought to spend more time on that.

Cookies, lemon-flavoured madeleines, truffles, apple muffins, yogurt cheesecakes, raspberry jellies, doughnuts . . .

Ashikawa brought them all in, one after another. Several types of cakes and cookies she made several times, but some, like truffles and doughnuts, only made one appearance. Harada and others praised her for them, saying she'd done well to make them the first time without any mistakes, and Ashikawa had smiled happily. Nitani knew that she only brought in things she had practised making many times successfully.

Shortly before lunch, or after three – this was when she usually handed out treats to everyone. Cookies and jellies, things that could be eaten quickly, were for before lunch, while more filling treats like madeleines or doughnuts were for 'afternoon snacks'. Afternoon snacks were welcomed by everyone who was working overtime. The less hungry you were, the easier work went.

Fuji suggested that everybody should chip in for the cost of ingredients, so twice a month a collection went round, taking 1,000 yen from employees and 300 yen from part-timers, which was handed over to Ashikawa. She had hesitated at first, saying, 'I can't take this!' But after Harada had said, 'It's meant to cover everything you've already made too, so take it, dear,' she accepted the money, held in a company envelope, with a bright smile. 'I'm going to use this to make even more delicious things than ever!' she said, clenching her fist, as if cheering herself on.

Strawberry shortcake, grilled bananas, chocolate and marshmallow muffins, pumpkin pie, sweet potatoes, warabi mochi, crème caramels . . .

He hated anything you had to eat on the spot. You had to eat it with everyone. Take the banana cookies – she'd said she hadn't had time to individually wrap them, so they were all in a big box, which everyone lined up in front of and she handed them a few each. She put a tissue on each person's palm, then, with a gloved hand, put the cookies on top. It reminded him of a soup kitchen. Of course this was different, but still. The only thing in common was queuing up to get food. And this wasn't food you needed to eat to live. I hate unnecessary food, Nitani thought, though every evening he had snacks while he drank beer.

The madeleines or doughnuts that she individually wrapped, or cakes that could be served on plates, those he liked. 'I'll eat it later,' he could say. 'My little reward for doing overtime.' I hear you, someone would say back in the same tone, but they were usually already eating theirs right then and there, so Nitani always wondered what exactly they thought they heard.

After quitting time when the part-timers had left, Ashikawa had left, then another one or two people had gone home, and Fuji and Oshio were gone too, when nobody was around to see, Nitani would take out the treat Ashikawa had made, his 'little reward for doing overtime', and throw it away. Sometimes he crushed it with his hand or threw it into a plastic bag and set it under his desk, then stomped on it with his foot.

'Got a moment?'

Nitani looked up and saw Oshio giving him a little wave. They stepped out into the hallway, which seemed quiet; when Nitani looked around he saw that everyone in the department next door had gone home already, and all he could see beyond the frosted glass pane in the door was a single emergency red light, blurrily distorted. Oshio's hair fell neatly at the line of her shoulder blades as she walked ahead of him.

She stopped and turned to face him in the empty elevator lobby. From her face it looked like something had happened. Tightly pursed lips, steady eyes under frowning eyebrows. Only her cheeks were slightly slack, as if they had let their guard down.

'Harada talked to me. She said she knows it's me throwing away Ashikawa's food.'

He imagined Harada's face, with a certain hardness in her eyes and mouth. A troubled expression on her face, not full of blame, but rather full of consideration for the other person, sure that there must have been some reason, though she would certainly get to the bottom of it. Nitani looked at Oshio. All the part-timers went home on time, so Harada must have cornered her at lunchtime or when they were alone together in the toilet or kitchen at some point.

'I told her it wasn't me, and she got even more suspicious, like, "Well, if it isn't you then why didn't you say, Is someone really doing that? Who would really do something so horrible?" I got a little angry and told her, "Look, my desk is next to Ashikawa's, right? I eat anything she gives me right away, which Ashikawa would be able to confirm if you asked her," which she seemed to take on board, for now at least. But she's right. I messed up. The first thing I should've done was ask if someone was really throwing her stuff away, like she said. Now she knows I already knew and I'm gonna get caught. Or . . . I don't know, you know what I mean.'

Nitani hadn't asked the right question in response either, though, had he. As usual Oshio's expression looked severe, though her voice was light, like she was inviting him to hang out.

Suddenly paranoid, Nitani turned around to look behind him but no one was there. He had not heard the office door open and close, so he knew he and Oshio were still the only ones there, but nevertheless, he kept looking over his shoulder.

'It's not what she gives me. I find some stuff she made in the bin, and I just take it out. Then I sneak over and put it on her desk.'

'When did this start?'

It was the first time Nitani had spoken in a while. His voice was calm. Just some trouble at the office. Confirming the timeline of events with a junior employee. Still unclear as to whether this was a mistake on someone's part. No point in raising his voice. Therefore his voice was indifferent: when did this start?

'Last month. The day we had that meeting at eight in the morning at the client's request. You remember. The day everyone came in at seven-thirty moaning about how it was too early. I got in first that day. I came in at six-thirty, got the key from the guard, set up the meeting room, then I ate a pastry I bought at a convenience store on my way in, and I went to throw away the rubbish from it in the bin in the hallway, not the one under my desk. I did that because I drank a carton of vegetable juice too, and there was still some vegetable . . . sludge at the bottom of the carton, and I thought that if it sat in the bin under my desk all day long it might start to stink. So, when I went to put it in the bin in the hallway, I saw that there was something in the bottom of the bin already. The cleaning people empty the bin in the hallway around eight every night. So I figured that someone who had worked late the night before had thrown away stuff from their dinner or something, but then I saw the whipped cream sticking inside the plastic bag, and I was like, "Wait," so I pulled it out of the bin.'

'That's a pretty big bin, too. I'm impressed you could reach the bottom.'

'Well, yeah. I held on to the rim of the bin with my left hand and stuck my whole right arm in, up to my shoulder, really all of it, and somehow I got it.'

Oshio extended her arm towards the floor to show him. Suddenly he remembered the story she'd told him about reaching in like that to save the cat. Maybe picking up fallen objects was her true calling.

'Inside the bag was a tart. The one she made with grapes on top, you remember? With the pure white cream that still tasted of grapes somehow. Oh, I guess since you didn't eat it you wouldn't know that. Though everybody talked about it. This cream tastes just like grapes, they said.'

Since you didn't eat it. Her face had looked severe again as she said those words. Nitani was slowly starting to feel like he was receiving a report on some misdoing by a third party that was nothing to do with him, something purely work-related, which neither he nor Oshio had any involvement in instigating. Staying silent he nodded slightly, engaging in a small deception, and urged her to continue.

'The cream was stuck to the bag, but the tart was still in good shape. Not a bite had been taken; two of the big grapes were still stuck on top. I put the basically perfect tart back in the plastic bag, squeezed out as much of the air from the bag as I could, pulled the opening together tightly, and put it on Ashikawa's desk. Then I took a piece of scrap paper from the pile by the printer and put that on top.'

'Then what did Ashikawa do?'

'She noticed right away when she came in, I think. Even without opening the bag she could tell from the cream sticking to it, and from the way it felt when she picked it up, she must've known it was a tart from the day before. I was at my desk next to hers wondering what I should do, so I looked at her out of the corner of my eye. Ashikawa quietly put it in the bin underneath her own desk; she didn't look around, she just went on like usual. She listened to one of Fuji's boring stories as she turned on her computer, then got some tea out of the fridge, walked back over towards me and said something about how early it was and how tired everyone must be.'

Oshio furrowed her brows and whispered, 'Isn't that kind of weird?'

Then she continued: 'Afterwards, two more times, I put things I'd found in the bin on her desk. Cheesecake and a berry muffin. The cheesecake and the muffin were both untouched too, so much so it wouldn't have seemed strange to take them out of their bags and eat them, if they hadn't been in the bin. Both those times I found them late at night, so I put them in my desk drawer, and then I put them on her desk the next morning, when nobody else was in yet.'

He knew he was supposed to ask her why she'd done that. He found himself thinking, unrelatedly: I like this side of her better than when she smiles, that sincere look on her face as she talks like she's sharing a normal work update, rather than confessing her wrongdoings.

'Apparently, Harada had seen it before Ashikawa came in to work. She'd wondered what was on Ashikawa's desk, so she took off the paper, and saw that inside the crumpled-up bag was clearly something she'd made. I don't know how she concluded from that that it was me who had thrown it out, though. I guess she knows somehow that I hate Ashikawa. It just sucks to think that the part-timers are all talking about me like that.'

Oshio sighed. He waited for her to go on, but that seemed to be where the story ended. Nitani looked behind him once more to confirm that nobody else was in the hall, then he spoke.

'I'm not the one who threw those ones out.'

Oshio knitted her brows and stared at Nitani. No way, her eyes said. He stared right back into her eyes. She and I are similar at heart, but the other parts that make us up are completely different, so I suppose we'll always end up heading in opposite directions, he thought.

'The ones I throw away, I crush them to a pulp, so if they were still in one piece, that wasn't me. And if you didn't throw them away either, then that means someone else is fed up too.'

Oshio's eyes widened.

'I hadn't even considered that possibility. I thought it had to be you . . . though I guess when you think about it, it's not so crazy after all.' She paused, then muttered, sounding bored, 'Well, enough of that, I guess.'

She suddenly changed the subject to something about work, checking on the progress of something that needed to be done urgently, then casually started walking off towards the office. They walked back through the door together as they came to a compromise about how far they had to get tonight before they could go home. 'Then let's try to get this wrapped up in two hours,' Nitani said, as they each returned to their desks.

'But I wanted to go home in an hour,' Fuji grumbled.

'Same,' added another male employee; when everyone had shut their mouths, all that remained was the sound of keyboards clattering.

Nitani's phone vibrated in his pocket, and when he took it out, he saw some notifications from the group chat from his university literature class. He saw his name in the message preview, and though he'd meant to read the messages once he got home, he accidentally pressed 'view'.

'Hey Nitani, I finally read that book you recommended to me at uni.'

There was a picture of a book and a cup of coffee on top of a table.

'Took you long enough lol'

'Nah I get it. Sometimes it takes a few years to get to the point where you can read something'

The conversation continued popping up.

'It was good too, so if you have any other recs for me lemme know. Also hey are you even alive, man?'

He turned off the screen and put his phone back in his pocket. Three or four times it vibrated to notify him that a new message had been received, and then it went silent.

Soon weekdays and Saturdays weren't enough to keep up, so they started to work on Sundays too. On the weekend, they didn't stay as late as during the week; around seven or eight, he would leave work and go for a drink with Oshio or some of the others. Ashikawa was not among those who worked weekends, and since Nitani was late getting home, she no longer came over to stay at the weekend.

Once, she had asked him if she could bake at his house instead, but he didn't have an oven, nor any scales for measuring flour or sugar, not even any tablespoons or teaspoons. He had a bowl, but no spatula or one of those silvery wire things tied into a bundle on a stick. I doubt you'd be able to make anything, he said. Ashikawa might have replied that with a little ingenuity she could make it work, but Nitani's irritation had not so much peeked through his words as practically leapt out from behind them, so all she said was, 'That's too bad.' Nitani imagined the oppressively sweet, heavy syrupiness he smelled every time he passed by the bakery in his neighbourhood, that sugary smell that shoved its way inside him from his nose down to the bottom of his stomach and sank its claws into his heart and took hold of him, filling his own flat. That alone, he felt, was a reason they could not be together.

Instead of staying over on the weekend, Ashikawa started to come over to cook dinner a few times a month. Nitani worked four hours later than she did, so when he got home, steaming hot food was waiting for him, which Ashikawa stayed to make sure that he had eaten, then went home. He spent a short time with her. She looked at the news on her phone and remarked how such-and-such actor and such-and-such pop star had got married; she looked at a clothing website on his laptop and said this skirt looked cute but did not buy it; they watched a travel show and she said she wanted to go to the seaside but she hated swimming, but she still wanted to go, but no. These fragments piled up. Why does she come to my house so often and feed me? Is this what a relationship is? Nitani wasn't sure. Though his stomach was always full, whenever Ashikawa left, he couldn't stop himself from making and eating pot noodles.

After work was over, he stopped by a convenience store, then returned to his darkened flat. He washed his hands and filled the kettle. While the water came to a boil he changed into his loungewear, then poured the water into the instant soup and heated up the onigiri in the microwave for fifteen seconds only. His phone vibrated. It was a text from Ashikawa.

'Hope the rest of work wasn't too bad. Sorry to bother you this late, but I just wanted to tell you to eat something proper that's good for you, like miso soup!'

Reflexively, Nitani stood up and dumped the freshly made cup of soup with spinach in it down the kitchen sink. He picked a pot noodle from the stacks on top of the refrigerator, a limited-edition fatty tonkotsu one, and poured hot water in it. There wasn't enough water left in the kettle, but he couldn't be bothered to boil it again, so he just put the lid over it as it was. He felt a chill in his stomach. Only things that are not proper and good for me can warm me, Nitani thought as he stared at the steam escaping around the edges of the lid of the pot noodle.

Tell me all you like that eating a proper meal means taking care of myself and that eating pot noodles and ready-made side dishes is like self-abuse, but would working, doing overtime, going to the supermarket before it closes at ten, then making and eating dinner really be a better way to take care of myself? Just cut some vegetables and simmer them in broth with some meat – oh please. I don't want to eat that, it wouldn't satisfy me, because I'd still need some rice or noodles, and then at the very least, I'd have to wash the pot, my bowl, teacup, glass, chopsticks, knife and cutting board. Cook, eat, wash up, and before you know it an hour's gone by. I only have two hours after getting home before I have to go to sleep, and if I use one hour on eating, then in the remaining hour I have to take a bath and brush my teeth, then I only have half an hour to live my life! Would you still eat then? For your body? For your health? That's not eating to live, is it? Telling me to eat something proper, to take care of myself, to me that's an attack, however you want to say it.

After three minutes, he opened the pot noodle and added in the soup packet. The sticky fat floated on the surface, not fully dissolving in the hot water. When he stuck his disposable chopsticks in, the noodles felt too hard, and he realised that this brand took five minutes to cook instead of three, but he couldn't be bothered anymore, so he forced the noodles to separate and slurped it all down together with the clumpy soup, feeling nothing but heat.

'You look like you've gained a little weight,' Oshio told him on the way to a nearby izakaya after work. Today was the first day back at work after the holidays, and everyone was supposed to finish work at six and gather at an izakaya to celebrate the new year together.

They were still working overtime, but they'd been able to have a few days off from New Year's Eve to the third of January, and Nitani had gone back to his parents'. When he went to visit the nursing home where his grandmother lived, she told him, as always, that she wanted to live to meet her great-grandchildren, and he had told her, to encourage her, 'No great-grandchildren yet, but I am seeing someone now. We might get married someday soon,' to which his grandmother had beamed that she could wait. On the way home, in their father's car, his sister had asked Nitani what his girlfriend was like, which he deflected by saying, 'I just said that because of grandma – I'm not getting married any time soon,' to which she continued, 'I don't care about that. But it's you, so I'm guessing she's a nice girl who smiles a lot and doesn't assert herself.' He nodded and said yeah, pretty much, and his sister, looking satisfied, had said, 'Good. She'll make the perfect sister-in-law.' He knew his mother, sitting in the passenger seat, had listened to every word but said nothing.

Ashikawa had told him in advance that she would be with family for the first three days of the year, so on the night of the second he went back to his own flat and relaxed. He went to the supermarket once to buy instant food and ready-made New Year's food that had been discounted. Otherwise, he did not leave his flat; he let some videos play on his laptop without watching them and read books.

'Guess it's all that holiday food,' said Nitani, while thinking to himself that wasn't true at all. The weight he'd put on wasn't from overindulging at the end of the year. He'd gained it gradually over the last six months. It wasn't just because work had been busy and he'd been eating late at night, either. Because he'd lived under those conditions last year and the year before at his former branch. In his mind, he saw Ashikawa's face as she slept and a broth with globs of fat floating in it. And the white plastic container it was in as well.

'Imagine what you'd be like if you got fat and stopped taking care of yourself.'

He was still at the receiving end of Oshio's blunt laughter when they arrived at the izakaya. They were led to a Japanese-style room with a long, low table on one side and though they were initially jammed in at the end far from the management, by the time they'd almost finished eating the duck hot pot served as part of the set party menu, the branch manager had wound up at a seat not too far from their end of the table with Ashikawa and another female employee, both speaking in high spirits, in tune with the boss's drunken laughter. Fuji sat next to Ashikawa, across from the boss. His face was bright red. Ashikawa was blotting the water that had melted from the ice that had landed on the knee of Fuji's suit trousers when he'd accidentally knocked over a glass with his elbow. The phrase 'sacrificial lamb' came to Nitani's mind, but it wasn't an unusual sight either.

Nitani and another young male employee settled into seats near the head of the table, now largely vacated. In front of Nitani was a bowl of half-eaten rice porridge and a pair of chopsticks he couldn't tell if someone had used. He pushed them aside and asked the waiter for a beer. 'Still on the beer?' asked the guy sitting in front of him, impressed. His voice was especially loud, perhaps because of the sake he'd been drinking since halfway through the party. Just as Nitani was about to call out to the waiter and ask for a glass of water too, he heard a shriek. It was not a scream. Each sound of it was pronounced exactly, 'E-e-k!' with the same cheerful tone as when Ashikawa brought in some treats, but it also had a strange darkness to it. Everyone at Nitani's end of the table turned to look instantly. Fuji was hugging Ashikawa. No, that wasn't it. Ashikawa was hugging Fuji.

'What?' someone behind him whispered. He knew without turning around that it was Oshio's voice. She was sitting at a table with the part-timers, all women, chatting away; Oshio said again, in a clearly disgusted voice, 'Ugh, what are they doing?'

Ashikawa, kneeling on the tatami mat floor, was hugging Fuji, who was sitting with his feet in the recess under the low table. The hug was gentle, not tight. Though he didn't really know what difference that made. Fuji's head was resting on Ashikawa's outstretched arms. His face was hidden behind her arm, but he could see Ashikawa's face. Her gaze was directed at the top of Fuji's head. 'That must've been tough,' he heard her say. Where does a voice that kind even come from, he wondered. It was the voice of someone saying, I forgive you. One that could only be wielded by someone who had received forgiveness. Fuji nodded silently. Did his head just hit her chest when he did that? Nitani started feeling sick. The duck hot pot quivered in his stomach.

'Apparently Fuji's wife left him,' Harada, sitting at the same table as Oshio, explained in a voice loud enough that even Nitani and the others near him could hear. 'They had a fight because she didn't want to go to his parents' house together for the holidays, and she just walked out. Didn't hear from her at all over the holidays. He even went to her family's place, but she wouldn't come out to see him.'

Nitani was surprised at how much information they'd gathered just gabbing away at a table full of women. Everyone nodded and said things like, 'Oh, so *that's* what his deal is.'

'Now that you mention it, he did seem pretty off today,' someone else said, but Nitani hadn't noticed a thing. He thought Fuji had been the same as always, and anyway, there was something strange about thinking you had to have a reason to be obviously down at work.

'But then why is Ashikawa hugging him?'

That was Oshio. Her face looked like she'd just stepped on a large insect barefoot.

'Because he's drunk and he kept going on and on,

like, "I'm so sad, I need a hug, I'm so sad." I guess she couldn't just sit there and do nothing? I mean, she's so nice.'

The part-timers made sympathetic noises, then suddenly, having lost interest, they returned to their original chatter. The guy sitting across from Nitani also started talking about something else, drawing him back into the conversation with a 'Hey'; as he turned his head back his eyes met Oshio's, and he thought that she would turn away from looking at him, just like she always did when they caught each other's eyes at work, but instead she stared, leaving him no choice but to be the one to look away first.

As he chatted with the people around him, he casually stole a glance down at the other end of the room; Ashikawa had already settled back down into a normal position, and Fuji was turned talking to the boss as if nothing had happened.

They brought out almond tofu for dessert. Nitani took a spoonful of it but did not put it into his mouth. He pushed his dish behind the hot pot, as if to hide it.

It happened two days after the party. Right after lunch was over, when everyone from the boss to the part-timers was all gathered, Fuji said to the branch manager,

'May I say something?' Harada was standing right behind him. The branch manager looked up; Fuji looked around the room then asked, loud enough for all to hear, 'Is that all right with everyone?' Everyone looked at him. Judging from Fuji's restrained tone of voice, they guessed that it couldn't be anything good; everyone waited quietly for him to speak.

'I really would rather not have to talk about this in front of everyone, but I have tried to handle this privately and things did not improve, or rather they didn't stop, so I'm afraid I have no choice but to bring it up like this.'

Fuji looked around at everyone as he finished his sentence, then he turned to look at the branch manager and apologised again in a low voice. The boss nodded, a dubious look on his face. It didn't seem they had discussed this previously.

'As you all know, Ashikawa always brings in treats for everyone, but someone in this office has been bagging them up like garbage and putting them on Ashikawa's desk.'

Everyone started murmuring: whoa, what, that's awful. Nitani heard someone gasp, then realised the sound had come from his own throat; a strangely calm feeling came over him. He twisted his head to look at Oshio, who was staring straight at Fuji. Ashikawa, next to him, averted her gaze and looked down at her own hands, but feeling everyone's eyes on her, pulled her slender shoulders up and in and gently turned her downcast face towards Fuji. Fuji caught her eyes and nodded firmly. As if to say: don't worry, leave it to me.

'It happened again today. You remember the chestnut cakes Ashikawa made and gave everyone yesterday. This morning, there was a bag, a crumpled-up plastic bag, with one in it on her desk.'

'What on earth,' the boss said in a low voice. 'Do you know who it is? You don't have to say it here. Come see me later,' he said, pointing to the conference room in the back.

'I do know who it is, but I'll refrain from saying their name here. I have warned the person responsible directly before. If you don't want to eat what she makes, then don't eat it. If you don't like sweet things, you just need to tell Ashikawa you don't want any – that's all you have to do.'

Everyone nodded silently.

'But taking what she's made and putting it in a bag on her desk, that's just horrible. Ashikawa makes treats for us all, to give us a little pick-me-up, out of the kindness of her heart, and someone chooses to attack her for it. She says that this has been going on since last autumn. Because she's so nice, at first she assumed that someone was doing it to return things they couldn't eat to her. But if that was your intention, you wouldn't use a crumpled-up bag. Harada was the one who noticed something was wrong.'

Fuji looked at Harada, who was standing next to him.

'When Harada asked Ashikawa what had happened, she told her everything. Harada was shocked that someone would do something so horrible and told me about it. It is unforgivable. Ashikawa told me, "If someone wants to hurt me I wish they'd find another way. There are too many people in this world who don't have enough to eat, so I wish they wouldn't waste food like this." Doing something so awful to someone with such a beautiful heart is – really, it's unforgivable.'

Everyone nodded again. 'Awful,' someone whispered.

Fuji had stared at Oshio's face from start to finish as he spoke.

Now Nitani and everyone else's eyes turned to Oshio too. They peeked at her hesitantly. Oshio's face had turned pale. Her expression had crumbled; her eyes were no longer turned towards Fuji but towards the back of Ashikawa, sitting in the seat next to her, who now had turned her body fully towards Fuji, her gaze downward. 'She's staring at her,' Harada muttered. It was more a statement of amazement than reproach. Her voice had been quiet, but since she was standing next to Fuji, everyone had heard her. Oshio's cheeks twitched, yet her gaze did not waver from Ashikawa.

The boss, Fuji and Harada went into another room to talk, and not long after, Ashikawa was asked to come in too. After fifteen or twenty minutes of talking, they each returned to their work, but shortly afterwards, when Oshio went out into the corridor, the boss silently followed her.

When Oshio walked out, nobody said anything, but they all stopped working, exchanging meaningful glances. One of the female part-timers asked Ashikawa if she was all right; she nodded feebly. 'It's awful, just awful,' said Harada. Fuji sighed loudly through his nose and crossed his arms.

About half an hour later, the boss returned to his desk, followed a few minutes after by Oshio. Neither said anything. Nobody else said a word either; only the sound of keys tapping echoed in the oppressive atmosphere. Not long after, someone groaned, and when Nitani snapped his head up to look, he saw Oshio with both hands pressed to her mouth. Her body was trembling from the effort. 'Somebody—' Harada said, coming to her feet, and Nitani quickly ran to the kitchen and grabbed a plastic bag. He handed it to

Oshio gently so as not to startle her. She looked up at him, her eyes twitching in her pale face, and nodded slightly. Nitani thought she would take the bag and leave the room, but she stayed sitting still in her chair. Maybe it's so bad she can't get up to go to the bathroom, he thought; nearly five minutes later, she stood up suddenly.

'I'm OK.' She turned to the people around her. 'Sorry for worrying you. I'm fine,' she said. Everyone nodded vaguely. Nobody had said anything about being worried. Oshio crumpled up the plastic bag that she held in her hand.

'I'm fine. I didn't throw up,' she said.

The worst of the work was done and though they were a little busy towards the end of the fiscal year, things had calmed down a little. They no longer had to work weekends, and even on weekdays people could leave at seven; Ashikawa started spending weekends at Nitani's flat again. She brought treats in to work less often, and what she brought was more conventional, like cookies and pound cake, things that weren't too elaborate to make on a weeknight.

'You know, you don't have to come over every weekend – take some time and bake on your own if you want sometimes,' Nitani said.

Ashikawa's eyes leapt, filled with happiness.

'But once I get married, I won't be able to just bake all the time.'

Nitani didn't think that was true, but he didn't know what to say to Ashikawa, who seemed to believe it. If she didn't think she would be able to do what she wanted after marriage, then perhaps whoever she married wouldn't either. Instead of saying anything, he ventured a smile; in response, the corners of Ashikawa's mouth lifted a few millimetres higher.

April's personnel changes were announced, and Nitani was to be moved to another branch in Chiba. It would take two and a half hours one way to commute there from his current flat. It was annoying, but he had no choice but to move again.

Only a few of the female part-timers reacted with surprise; all the other employees had expected that this would happen, and rumours quickly started going around about what so-and-so at that other branch had done.

'It's because I'm young and they can't move anybody else there,' Nitani explained to the part-timers.

'It's you-know-who's fault,' said Harada, her voice pointed. In mid-February, long before Nitani's transfer had been announced, the boss had told the entire staff that Oshio was leaving, and everyone seemed to have decided that Nitani was being transferred because Oshio, who had been at their branch for five years, had been meant to go, so someone else had to take the transfer instead. Ever since the incident, people had had it in for Oshio, whispering about her in the office, but Nitani thought that if his transfer had to be somebody's fault, it was Ashikawa's, not Oshio's.

Based on number of years served and work responsibilities, Ashikawa should've been the one transferred, not Oshio, but the boss and Fuji had put a stop to her transfer. Or rather, they were putting a stop to it, since before Nitani had arrived at that branch and going forwards. Apparently they had decided she needed to be protected here. Or at least that's what he'd heard from Ashikawa. She'd told him how wonderful it was; if she could just stay at that office, she'd never have to move out of her parents'.

Oshio had lost and Ashikawa had won. It was a battle of strength versus weakness disguised as a match of right and wrong. Naturally, the weaker one had won. That was how it always was.

Oshio's official last day was at the end of March, but her last day in the office would be the third of March, because she was going to take all her remaining leave. In the toilets, Fuji grumbled to him, 'Normally, if you say you're going to use up your leave, you only take half of it. Nobody uses it all.' This was news to Nitani. If I quit there's no way I wouldn't take it all, he thought, but then he also felt sure he'd keep working there until retirement anyway. He had thirty years until he could retire. If the retirement age was extended to sixty-five or seventy, that'd make it nearly forty years. A long time. Too long, but not so much so that it daunted him any longer. Eat, sleep, get up, eat – time would pass like that before he even realised.

'So you and Ashikawa'll be far apart now, huh.'

Finally someone had actually mentioned her name to him. 'Well, I'm sure we'll still see each other on weekends,' Nitani said, realising flatly as he spoke that what he said was true.

'You know, it's too bad. Wish we could've worked together a little longer.'

Fuji slapped Nitani on the shoulder and walked out of the bathroom.

Immediately after the announcements that Oshio was leaving and Nitani would be transferred, the two of them went out drinking together. That was the last time Nitani would see Oshio one-on-one.

Oshio said that she wanted to eat hot pot, so they went to a snug old-school izakaya in a back alley. Oshio ordered duck; when Nitani asked, 'That's what we had at the New Year's party, right? You like it?' Oshio pursed her lips and said, 'That was really bad. Not the food itself necessarily but anything you eat with everyone from work just feels gross. I like duck but that was just awful. So I want a do-over.'

'I think I get it. It's usually bad whenever you eat with lots of people.'

As he spoke, memories of high school came to mind.

'Sometimes, when we were done with after-school clubs in high school, fifteen or so of us would go out for ramen, which I fucking hated. With that many people you always wind up somewhere gross with no other customers, because they only care that it's cheap and the portions are big, and everybody keeps saying how good it is while they're eating, but I really hated it, especially when everyone was shouting at each other with food in their mouths. The place where we'd go was pretty far, about half an hour one way by bike, so we'd be pedalling away in a big line down the road, which actually I liked, so it kind of saves it for me because all in all it's a nice memory.'

'Oh, yeah, we did that too – on the way home from club meetings we'd all go eat crêpes. Running around in big groups like that is such a teenage thing to do, right?'

Nitani was caught off-guard by how jovially Oshio had taken his story. He nodded for lack of anything to say, but he thought to himself that that hadn't been quite what he meant. *Boys need to eat.* The words suddenly rang in his mind. An older woman's voice. It could've been his mother's voice or grandmother's, or Harada's, or his old homeroom teacher's, or any number of other middle-aged women he'd known. Everybody finished an extra-large ramen, even drinking all the soup, but he didn't really like eating that much food. But he never could say that. At times like that, he always heard those words playing in his head. *Boys need to eat. Eat up and grow strong.*

'Leave it to me,' Oshio said, taking charge of the cooking to make sure that her do-over went as she wanted; she served the hot pot up to both of them, the ingredients cooked just right.

'Mm, that's how it should be. That's good.' Oshio seemed satisfied, eating more vegetables than meat, saying that the best part of it was cabbage cooked in the rich duck fat. They ordered white rice and raw eggs to turn the remains into rice porridge and finished the whole thing, including the soup. They sighed; their breaths were warm.

'Everything tastes good when I eat it with you,' Oshio said, smiling. She didn't smile and then say it; it was as if while speaking, her cheeks and the corners of her eyes shifted into a smile due to the movement of her lips.

'You almost never talk about what you're eating, Nitani, and I don't anymore either. I don't need to say, "Wow, this is good", or "Oh, it's so light and fluffy", or any of that stuff now – if it tastes good then I can just think that to myself and it's fine. I always felt I was just really bad at sharing that feeling of enjoying food with others. Well, I did suck at it, but I was good at pretending that I was on the same page as everyone else. Even if you're all eating the same thing, everyone's tastes are different – some people like things sweet or spicy – but still everyone has to say, "Wow, this is great", and I realised that's the thing that really gets me. When I eat with you, though, I don't feel like that at all. I feel like I'm eating alone. But with someone to talk to. So I feel sad. That we won't be going to eat together again. You're being transferred to Chiba, aren't you? That's so far.'

She pursed her lips. 'And I'm going to be busier too,' she said. 'A friend of mine from cheerleading started her own company where people can hire cheerleaders or other performers for events. I'm going to be responsible for general affairs in the administrative department . . . is what I think she said, but it's a small company so I imagine I'll wind up doing a bit of everything. I'll probably have to go to some events too, I guess.'

'And are you going to cheer too?'

'No way,' she said, and laughed.

The waiter brought over their hot tea. Oshio picked hers up, wrapping both hands around the cup, warming her palms. Vestiges of steam rose from the hotpot, though the burner was off beneath it. The heating in the restaurant was on as well, yet Oshio looked as if she were somewhere tremendously cold.

'But wherever I go I'll be the same. Or I might try to tell myself I've changed, but I won't have. There's something the coach always used to say when I was on the cheerleading squad. "People who can't cheer for themselves can't cheer for others." I never got what she meant. I mean, it's so easy to just tell someone they can do it, right? Encouraging yourself is much harder. I still kind of feel that way, but it's weird, because now I've ended up working at a company dispatching cheerleaders-for-hire. I guess just having another job lined up is me encouraging myself, in a way.'

Nitani thought he understood but said nothing, sensing that if he said he got it, she'd think he didn't. Just as they were about to leave, he asked, 'So it was you who took the cakes out of the bin and put them on Ashikawa's desk, then?' She still had an expression on her face as if she were somewhere cold and alone.

'I think we're losing the ability to help each other. We're letting go of things we once had. Because it's easier to live that way. As an adult. And the fact that what you eat alone tastes better than what you eat with other people is part of that. I don't think you have to feel like the food you share with others is delicious in order to live meaningfully.'

Nitani pointed at himself, then said something he hadn't planned on saying.

'The day they stitched you up because someone had taken a cake out of the bin and put it on her desk again – that was me.'

As he spoke, he already regretted it, but he continued.

'And I think she must've known too. After all, the cakes that were put on her desk back in the autumn weren't smashed up, but that one was different – it had been destroyed, so she must've realised someone else had done it.'

Oshio put her hand to her mouth and looked lost in thought for a moment, then slowly shook her head side to side.

'It doesn't matter,' she said. 'I'm the one who asked if you wanted to bully her in the first place anyway.'

Once they had left the restaurant all the warmth built up in their bodies dissipated in an instant. Instinctively Nitani drew in his shoulders and wrapped his coat tighter around him, while Oshio, who had borne the look of someone adrift in the frigid far north while they were inside, now looked quite unbothered as she walked off briskly towards the station.

A leaving party to mark Nitani's transfer and Oshio's resignation was to be held on the third of March, Oshio's last day in the office. One of the part-timers said she couldn't come because she was going to celebrate Girls' Day with her young daughter instead, so she gave them each a pretty box of sweets. The boxes were small enough to fit in the palm of a hand; inside were biscuits, she said. They sported the name of a famous bakery in Tokyo. 'I'm sure they're no match for what Ashikawa makes, though,' she said, then looked at Oshio in alarm and ended the conversation, hurrying back to her desk. It was clear she hadn't meant to be snide – if anything, she'd probably meant to flatter Nitani, who, office rumour had it, was dating Ashikawa. Rather than sigh, Oshio smiled slightly.

Nitani opened his box later that afternoon when he started to feel a little peckish. There were only four biscuits inside: two chocolate, two vanilla. He gobbled them up quickly, leaving nothing in the box but the packet of desiccant. The biscuits were all the same size, the same shape. He imagined they were made in a real kitchen by pâtissiers wearing hats, masks and aprons.

The thought filled him with a sense of relief. This was proper food, made by professionals who didn't know the faces of the people who would eat it. On his way to make some copies, he passed near the desk of the woman who'd given them to him and said, 'Those were great.' As she replied that she was glad, she looked somewhat surprised.

'I was right, you do like to eat sweets late in the day. Lucky for you, you've always got Ashikawa's baking here as a little reward for doing overtime.'

He smiled back as if to say, that's so true, dodging the comment. Slowly he turned away and headed towards the copier, letting the conversation die. Ashikawa looked on from across her desk. The taste of the biscuits still lingered in his mouth.

As it neared time for everyone to finish up for the day and head to the restaurant they'd booked, Oshio went up to the manager's desk and said, smoothly, 'I'm very sorry, but I have a terrible headache. I'm sure you've all gone to a lot of trouble, but I'm afraid I'm not going to the party. Thank you for all you've done for me over the years. What I've learned here will help me to do the best I can. Maybe we'll cross paths again someday. I hope you'll think well of me then,' before giving a quick bow.

Unable to object, the manager mumbled in response, 'Oh yes, if you're not feeling well then that's that, though it is a shame.' Then he looked out across the department. 'At least say goodbye to everyone who's still here,' he urged her. Almost all the permanent staff were still there. Only Ashikawa had left right on the dot with the part-timers to go ahead to the restaurant.

Oshio looked around at everyone. 'It's been great working with you all,' she said, loudly. She seemed rather happy. 'I know you've planned a leaving party and everything, but I'm not feeling well,' she explained. 'But I kind of didn't want to go anyway, so good thing I've got this headache, I guess. Anyway, I imagine you'll all have a better time if the party's just for Nitani, right?' Startled gasps went around the room.

'I don't mean to be sarcastic; it's just what I'm really thinking. I mean, it's my last day, so why say something I don't mean, right? And I'm not trying to make a nasty last speech and then run away, either. I just want to quit lying. That's all. I really do have a headache. I get migraines – my head always hurts. I usually try to power through it and come into the office or go out for drinks after work, or I did, but hey, I'm quitting, so why push myself now? Anyway, I just wanted to express my appreciation. I've learned a lot from you all. Thanks for everything.'

Some sparse and scattered applause sounded, then died out before it could grow much louder. People looked around at each other, unsure how to respond.

As they did, Oshio adjusted her clothes, put her bag on her shoulder, slung her coat over her arm, then turned to the man who had organised the leaving party and thrust an envelope into his hands. 'Here's my contribution towards tonight's bill,' she said.

'Oh, you don't need to do that.'

She ignored his refusal.

'Right, well, thanks again, guys.' She bowed her head towards everyone once more, then turned and left.

The venue for the leaving party was a new Italian restaurant; first they brought out prosciutto quiche, followed by mushrooms al aglio, fried whitebait, risotto in a tomato cream, and so on. Nitani had been offered wine, but he drank beer all night instead. Something in a green bottle, apparently an Italian beer. He couldn't tell what made it any different to Japanese beer. They'd reserved the back half of the restaurant, and Nitani had been made to sit in the very middle. Everyone else kept rotating to sit and talk to him, so he stayed seated the whole time. He just wanted to get home as soon as possible and eat a pot noodle.

Soon after they'd all finished their risotto, Ashikawa appeared carrying a large cake. Instead of candles it was adorned with little fireworks crackling and giving off sparks. Wow, said the whole room except for Nitani. Harada said, 'Clear a space there,' pointing in front of him, and the people sitting around Nitani quickly gathered plates from the table and made room. Ashikawa set the cake down gently. A little plaque on the cake read, 'Thank you, Nitani and Oshio!'

'She made it all herself, even that plaque!' Harada, seeming impressed, shouted, conveying the information to everyone; Ashikawa smiled shyly. The glare of the fireworks hurt Nitani's eyes. 'Amazing,' he murmured. 'Just amazing. How do you even make something like that?'

Someone thoughtfully got up from the seat next to Nitani and sat Ashikawa down there instead. They got a waiter to take a group photo. The cake was right in the centre of it, like the star of the show. Everyone got out their phones and took their own pictures of the cake too. It was decorated with white cream in the shape of a ribbon; the sides were frosted perfectly, not the slightest imperfection to be found. The light green plaque on top was surrounded with scattered flower petals. All kinds and colours of blooms. He remembered Ashikawa had said once that some flowers were edible. And how he'd thought then: is there nothing in this world you won't eat?

And that went for everyone, too. All trying to eat

anything good. More, more, whatever you've got – exhausting. Why does everything have to be celebrated with a cake? Mouths gooey and sticky with lumps of sugar, murmuring: ooh, this is so good, you guys. Why did everyone feel they had to gorge themselves like this?

Ashikawa took out the spent fireworks and cut the cake. She dished it up onto plates provided by the restaurant. The cake was doled out piece by piece. 'You get the biggest one,' she said, handing Nitani the piece with the plaque on it. At the edge of it, he could see a small fingerprint, probably hers.

'This is so good,' Nitani said as he ate. 'Wow, you really can bake. Oh, and there's fruit inside. No way, that's amazing. God, this is good. It's so sweet. You've gotta be a total genius, to make something like this. You can really taste the cream, wow. This is so, so incredible. Must be the best in the world.'

Cramming his mouth full of sponge cake, the cream coating the fronts and backs and in-betweens of his teeth, he ate. Each time he said wow, she smiled. Her face beamed as she smiled. She looked so delighted. 'Is that really what makes you happy?' he asked, his mouth full of cake, and she, still smiling, only responded with a 'Huh?'

'Wonder if we'll marry,' he said. Her eyes widened, having only heard the word 'marry'. The silver eyeshadow on her lids gleamed. The plump skin around her eyes quivered.

'I promise I'll make you good food every day,' she whispered, her voice sweet and cream-coated. Staring right at him, eyes unwavering. Her happy face mercilessly adorable.